THE DRUGS FARM

The police suspect an American hard-line drugs dealer escaped from custody to be in England and they know of the expensively organised release from a maximum security prison of an industrial chemist. Their investigations are hampered by their sheer innocence of the criminals' resources and capacity for corruption, even in the citadel of power. No wonder there seems little chance of uncovering the criminals' product — a dangerous and hallucinogenic drug — that could threaten the young everywhere.

P. A. FOXALL

THE DRUGS FARM

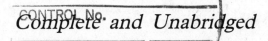

Complete and Unabridged

LINFORD
Leicester

First published in Great Britain in 1984 by
Robert Hale Limited
London

First Linford Edition
published 1999
by arrangement with
Robert Hale Limited
London

British Library CIP Data

Foxall, P. A. (Peter Augustus) *1923*–
    The drugs farm.—Large print ed.—
Linford mystery library
1. Detective and mystery stories
2. Large type books
I. Title
823.9'14 [F]

ISBN 0–7089–5459–6

Published by
F. A. Thorpe (Publishing) Ltd.
Anstey, Leicestershire .

Set by Words & Graphics Ltd.
Anstey, Leicestershire
Printed and bound in Great Britain by
T. J. International Ltd., Padstow, Cornwall

This book is printed on acid-free paper

1

Detective Inspector Jack Prosser of C11 (Criminal Intelligence) sat at his desk in Scotland Yard, frowning at a telex he'd just received from the National Crime Information Centre in Washington. It informed him that Bradley Chawton, wanted for Federal offences in drug peddling, armed robbery and attempted murder, had escaped from custody, slipped over the border into Canada, and was thought to be heading for London where he had associates in the criminal community. He was invariably armed and desperate.

'Please apprehend and hold for extradition.'

Accompanying the request was a set of finger prints and a teleprint photograph showing a square crew-cut head, a lean, wolfish face with bitter mouth and narrow, piercing eyes: definitely not the kind of face one would expect to see in church or at any other convivial gathering for peace and goodwill.

Jack Prosser called in his closest subordinate, Detective Sergeant Collins, and told him to set the machinery in motion: instant alert for Chawton at every point of entry in the country, and a circularised description with photographic likeness to every police force.

'Not that he'll look anything like this,' said Prosser. 'He'll probably have beard and mutton-chop whiskers and padding in his cheeks. He might even have had plastic surgery like Ronnie Biggs. We've got his dabs here, but they won't tell us anything until he leaves them at the scene of a crime.'

'Is that all then, guv?'

'No, not quite. According to FBI information Bradley Chawton has also been associated with an English business-man over there called Donald Aloysius Carrington. There wasn't enough evidence to charge Carrington with complicity in any of Chawton's crimes, but he was found to have outstayed his entry visa. So he's been declared persona non grata

and deported back here. That was over a
month ago, so he must be well settled in
by now, no doubt ready to give Chawton
a helping hand when he arrives.'

'Has this Carrington got form with
us?'

'I don't know yet. That's for you to
find out. Go and have a search through
Criminal Records and see if he's there.
I don't remember anyone by the name
of Carrington doing anything spectacular
while I've been on the Force. But if he's
an associate of this Bradley Chawton and
has got away with a few strokes over there
he's probably something more formidable
than a lower-league twister.'

DS Collins went away and was back
in less than an hour.

'Carrington has got form, guv'nor.
Fraud mainly, in the art and antiques
line, three convictions. His last rap was
in '79 and he got a four-years custodial,
of which he served two and a half.'

'What did he do?'

'He was running an art gallery, and
took an Arab oil sheik for a quarter of
a million with an expert reproduction

of an old master. Though the fake was exposed soon after the completion of the sale, the Arab never saw a penny of his money back. Carrington must have got it out straightaway to his Swiss account before he was nicked. It was a good rate of pay, tax free, for those two and a half years he did in stir. Which bloody idiot ever said that crime doesn't pay?'

'So Carrington is also a wealthy villain,' mused Prosser. 'Has he made any significant moves since he's been back?'

'That I couldn't tell you, guv. We've not had him in the Target Criminal File. He slunk back from the States without making any waves, and we'd never have noticed him if the Yanks hadn't tied him in with Bradley Chawton.'

'Well, you'd better locate Carrington soonest, and keep an eye on him vis-à-vis Chawton. If they worked together in the States they'll obviously team up here. The Yanks want Chawton back pretty badly, and Carrington has to be a good lead.'

'There's something else interesting I found out about Carrington, guv'nor.

4

He's got a very gifted wife in London.'

'Oh?'

'She lives in Chelsea under her maiden name, Elaine Cornford, and she's made quite a name for herself as a portrait painter to the wealthy. The word on her is that she's one of those nature-loving, bare-foot, bare-arsed Bohemiáns who screws around a lot and does her own thing, so that she's become chic and fashionable among the élite. For what it's worth there's a bit of a rumour going about in Society that Elaine is having it off with a Home Office minister, an up-and-coming young sprog by the name of Carvell. It's probably true, but it can't mean much in today's climate of free-wheeling sex.'

'Carvell at the Home Office? Wasn't he at the centre of some row whipped up by the newspapers some weeks ago? He deported some poor Polish Solidarity supporter who stowed away on an East German freighter, sent him back to Poland to face certain death in a Penal Battalion. About the same time he put out the red carpet for some black Rhodesian

5

terrorist who boasted about how many whites he'd killed during the war of liberation.'

'That's our boy, Digby Carvell. But it's done his career no harm at all. He was only following the national trend. He knows all the best people. He's wealthy and well connected and married to a Duke's daughter, so he's tipped as a political high-flyer.'

'Come to think of it, I've seen him referred to in the newspapers as Golden Boy. Hasn't he got a bit of a reputation as a womaniser, the House of Commons Groper?'

'That's him, guv, a real honcho in the sack. But he's fly enough not to get involved in any scandal that could hurt his political career. So if he's got a thing going with Elaine Cornford he must be pretty sure that her low-life husband is well bought off and not going to be a thorn in his side.'

'Did you find out whether this woman is still having anything to do with Carrington after his term of imprisonment and his tour of the States, or are they permanently estranged?'

'They've never been divorced is all we know for certain. But that doesn't get us anywhere unless Carrington gets married again and we can hang a bigamy rap on him.'

'You don't know if he's moved in with her in her Chelsea pad since his return?'

'No guv, but I can soon check it out.'

'Do that then, and make it a priority, even though he is only a shady art faker whom we wouldn't normally waste a lot of time on. It's the Chawton thing that really matters. Check at Passport Control on all male arrivals from North America, especially those coming in on a tourist visa. Once Chawton is here he'll probably try to stay as an illegal immigrant and go underground. So we have to nail him on arrival. We certainly don't want a sod like him getting cosy with some of our top-flight villains over here, and building up another empire for the Crime Busters to have to knock down. Carrington's money and Chawton's criminal know-how teamed up together could cause us a lot of grief.'

2

Not very long afterwards in a large terrace house in Wembley belonging to an American art dealer called Max Tordoff, who'd lived and worked in London for years, three plotters were holding a high policy meeting.

Donald Aloysius Carrington was a stocky black-haired man with the squat, muscular body of a middle-weight wrestler. He had coarse blunt features like a dog and his small black eyes were like steel poniards, humourless and touched with menace. A steely glow seemed to emanate from him, proclaiming his instant aggression towards the world even when he was among his own kind.

The second man was the American, Bradley Chawton, now masquerading under the name of Paul Rossiter and comfortably settled in the prosperous house of a London-based compatriot. He was small, tough and compact in physique with unhealthy sallow skin and very pale eyes totally devoid of lashes. He rapped out his words in a nasal snarl with overtones of the Bronx, where his formative years had been spent tangling with the law and blood-letting with street gangs. He'd learnt how to survive in the savagery of the bar-room brawl, the back-alley mêlée and the dockside ambush. His appearance had undergone a complete metamorphosis from that image of the snarling street fighter and caged animal which had come to Scotland Yard from the National Crime Information Centre. Chawton/Rossiter was now dressed in a neat grey two-piece suit, expertly cut and fitted by a smart London tailor. He wore heavy black-rimmed bifocals and a neatly trimmed beard which softened and civilised his face so that he looked more like a business executive or even an academic.

The third member of the syndicate was a giant who towered above them both, with a broad-shouldered rangy figure six feet four inches in height, as tough as old hickory. His face was grim, gaunt and menacing, tanned to the hue of dark mahogany by long exposure to the southern African sun. His scanty fair hair and eyebrows had been bleached nearly white by the same relentless power. Formerly a major in the élite Selous Scouts, the supreme hit-squad of the white Rhodesian army, he'd killed so many black guerrillas of ZANU and ZAPU during the seven-year long guerrilla war that the black hierarchy had put a thirty-thousand pound price on his head. When the white régime finally caved in and the Selous Scouts were vindictively disbanded, marked men like Henry Bernard Haldane had suddenly found themselves forced to melt chameleon-like into the earth like Nazi war criminals in 1945. Haldane had then done some mercenary soldiering in Angola and Mozambique, even though he was always bewildered as to who was fighting whom and for what purpose. But he found that the blacks were poor soldiers and worse paymasters, so in his quest for easy money he'd finally drifted to England to look up his old buddy Don Carrington, whom he'd known years before in South Africa when they were into the Illicit Diamond Brokerage together. A ruthless adventurer, prepared to go anywhere and do anything at a price, Haldane had come to London at a fortuitous time when Carrington was about to spread his wings in an ambitious criminal enterprise.

'The fuzz are still keeping that tail on me,' Carrington was saying. 'They're still watching Elaine's house round the clock. I could see the size of their feet from across the street.'

'Yeah,' said Chawton, 'I told you they don't give up easy. It's me they're after. The Feds will have tipped them off that you knew me over there. You didn't lead the bastards here, did you?'

'What do you take me for? I lost him in Selfridges, wearing a raincoat and carrying a briefcase when I went in; wearing a blonde wig and minus the raincoat and briefcase when I came out. I changed taxis twice and took a bus to the top of the road, but he wasn't with me.'

'You should moan!' grumbled the Selous Scout in his flat colonial English. 'What about me? They marked my bloody card at Heathrow Immigration Control. I'm only in this flaming country on a temporary visa that's up for renewal in eight days. They didn't welcome me here with open arms and a red carpet because I'm the wrong sodding colour. They'll probably ship me straight back to Zim-bab-we to have my throat cut on arrival by the lousy kaffirs.'

'Don't worry, Hal,' said Carrington cheerfully. 'I've got it in hand. With our pet eager beaver rooting for us in Queen Anne's Gate we'll get you a resident's permit that's valid for nine months and available for automatic renewal.'

'I hope to God you're right, Don. So what's this big money-spinning line you mentioned? Drugs?'

'What else?' said Chawton with a mirthless grin. 'The big fast-breeding money reactor of our time. The manufacture and marketing of, no less.'

'You mean a heroin processing plant right here in Merrie England?' said

Haldane, deeply impressed.

'Not heroin,' said Chawton emphatically.

'Why not? It's where the real money is, isn't it? You should know, pushing it in the States.'

'Heroin for the American market, OK. You got the big demand there and the marketing organisation well established down to every university campus and every nigger junkie den in Harlem. But it's a different ball game in Britain. They're all amateurs here, and there's not the money on the streets. Main-liners are counted in hundreds here, not hundreds of thousands. Then you've got these do-gooding quacks giving the stuff out on free prescription to the case-hardened addicts. You've got clinics getting 'em off it as fast as new junkies are turned on by substituting methodone. Besides, all the profitable heroin trade in this country is staked out already by the Chinese Triads with their Hong Kong connection. I may as well spell it out to you guys. I'm here to do business and open up a good permanent trading connection, not get mixed up in some half-assed gang war with the Triads.'

'Is that what you think as well, Don?' said Haldane, who'd already decided he wasn't all that fond of the cocky, fast-talking Yank.

'Brad's right,' said Carrington. 'We've both cased the British market and come up with the same answer. Heroin's not right for us here. The manufacturing process for chlorhydrate of diacetyl-morphine is too expensive. The advanced chemical equipment is difficult to get hold of without the risk of a security leak back to the fuzz. Then there's the long-standing difficulty of the supply of raw opium being brought in from overseas. The import of Turkish opium brought in by the civil airline crews is only a trickle, and the Drugs Squad is closing it off all the time. We couldn't depend on it to keep a processing plant going as efficiently and cost effectively as they do in Marseilles. So the big H is out.'

'What else did you have in mind?' said Haldane contemptuously. 'Blueys, goof balls, glue or paint-stripper?'

'LSD,' said Chawton promptly. 'Raw LSD in little tablets called microdots. Hallucinogenics to take 'em right out of their little heads so they can be Batman and Robin. That's the most cost-effective commodity for the British market. The main ingredient, ergotimine partrate can be got from pharmaceutical suppliers right here on base. We wouldn't even have to heist it if we were feeling honest.'

'The big attraction of the microdots is their saleability,' went on Carrington confidently. 'They're much cheaper to buy than a heroin fix, so they'll attract far more custom from the young trendy drug experimenters who like to ponce about with it but who'd run a mile at the prospect of main-lining on H. With LSD microdots there'll be a big fast turnover and a safer means of distribution through the disco/coffee-bar culture.'

'Damn right,' nodded Chawton approvingly.

'What's the profit margin like?' persisted Haldane.

15

'The microdots retail at ten pence each to the punters, and we sell to the middle men at five pence. From a kilo of ergotimine partrate we can make a million tablets, so even if we bought it legitimately at three-thousand quid a kilo we'd be getting sixteen hundred per cent profit on the outlay. The manufacturing process is simple and straight forward enough. The base for the tablets is a simple mixture of calcium carbonate and French chalk, and the manufacture is in two stages. The first part of the process takes four hours and the second about eight. And the sky's the limit for demand. The microdots are as good as sold before they're made.'

'All right,' conceded Haldane, 'you've done your homework and I'm convinced. I'll go along with it. Have you got the premises lined up for production?'

'Yes,' said Carrington with a self-satisfied grin. 'We've chosen a nice quiet backwater on a Northamptonshire farm where we're setting up the production laboratory, although the owner doesn't realise it yet. That's your part in the operation, Hal: production manager. You'll live there as a bona fide tenant farmer and supervise the manufacture of the microdots. Once a week you can deliver the whole production to Brad at some safe rendezvous to be arranged between yourselves. Brad will organise the marketing and distribution. But don't ever bring the microdots to this house under any circumstances, just in case the fuzz should get a line on it through Tordoff. If Brad doesn't show up at the collecting point for whatever reason, go back to the farm and get in touch by telephone.'

'OK. I think I can just about manage that,' agreed Haldane. 'But what kind of a set-up will I be ram-rodding at this farm? How many shifty buggers to keep an eye on?'

'Just one,' said Carrington. 'One industrial chemist is all it needs. We aim to get you a reliable man who can work on his own while you're away with the delivery of the finished product. He's also got to be completely trustworthy, so that he won't go shooting his mouth off in a pub when he's pissed, or pillow-talking to some whore.'

'And just where are you going to put your hand on that sort of treasure in the criminal community?' demanded Haldane ironically.

'Have you any progress to report, Brad?' said Carrington. 'You reckoned you had a good man lined up.'

'I thought I had,' replied Chawton peevishly, 'but the bastard reneged on me. He said the Drug Squad had busted him once before, and he wasn't happy working in this country. The real reason was he got a better offer for working a heroin processing plant in Marseilles. He thought he was slumming just making microdots out in the boondocks with sheep and cows for a social life, so he said 'up your ass'. It's no big problem though. Production chemists are common enough in the pharmaceutical companies. It's just a question of finding one with enough balls to take a risk for a piece of the action.'

'He's also got to be professional enough not to grass if anything goes wrong,' added Carrington. 'I've heard that the best man in his field is Terry Munton, known as the Gingerman. He's expensive, but he's a first-class chemist and absolutely loyal, a real professional. He'd never grass us if he was caught right at it among his test tubes.'

'So go ahead and sign the guy up if you're that sold on him,' said Chawton.

'Well, there's a slight problem with the Gingerman,' admitted Carrington with a frown. 'He's in Wormwood Scrubs just now. He's into a ten-year stretch for master-minding an LSD manufacturing operation from the labs at Imperial College, where he'd conned his way in as a lab technician.'

'Scrub him,' said Haldane laconically. 'He's no use to us in stir.'

'You have to admit he's single-minded about his job though.'

'And what the bloody hell good is that to us if the dumb loser's got himself in the slammer?' said Chawton contemptuously. 'Have you got anybody else in mind?'

'No, it's the Gingerman we want, so

we'll have him sprung,' said Carrington calmly.

'What! You're crazy.'

'No, I'm not. It's a dicey business springing from a Maximum Security nick, but it can be done. I've already been in touch with a team of escapologists who've worked the Scrubs before and know the lay-out.'

'Jesus!' muttered Chawton with grudging admiration. 'You had this figured out all along.'

'As I'm putting up most of the money to fund this operation it gives me a certain sense of responsibility to make it work,' replied Carrington bluntly. 'The man we have working the production line is really the key to the whole operation. He can foul us up and rat on us. But if he's depending on us for his continued freedom from the Scrubs, it'll give him the incentive to be loyal, hard working and conscientious.'

'That has to be good figuring anyway,' admitted Chawton approvingly.

'And what's the price for springing him?' said the Rhodesian.

'Twenty grand.'

'Christ!'

'Bloody hell!'

'Just regard it as an additional investment,' said Carrington smoothly. 'We'll get it all back and more with the first week's production. And it's not as if we have to run this project on a shoestring. It's always worth paying over the odds for the best qualified man.'

'He'd better be bloody well qualified for twenty grand,' said Haldane darkly. 'What's the agreement if they screw up and don't get him out?'

'Half the money down and half on completion when the Gingerman is safe over the wall. If they screw up we write off our ten grand and get back to head hunting for another chemist.'

'Well, in my opinion no bloody boffin is worth a hit-or-miss risk with ten grand,' said Haldane flatly.

'You're outvoted,' said Chawton sharply. 'I go along with Don on this. He knows the market and what kind of field we've got to choose from.'

'The chances of getting him out

21

are far better than fifty-fifty,' declared Carrington. 'The escape team drew me a picture showing how they reckon it can be done. There are one or two grey areas where things must take their chance. That's inevitable in such an operation, and that's why the price comes so high. But the probability is complete success, and the main thing going for us is the English Disease.'

'What's that?' said Chawton curiously.

'The English Disease is not, as you Yanks seem to think, snobbery or class mania or antiquity worship, or even strike-happy, bureaucratic, masochistic trade unionism. The real English Disease is a fatuous complacency bordering on the idiotic. And the higher you go up the social, political and Establishment ladder, the more fatuous it gets. When you come to the Bertie Woosters who run this country the complacency is absolutely unbelievable. So the English Disease must be really thriving in an Establishment fortress like Wormwood Scrubs, which is the most secure, the most prestigious, and after Dartmoor the most famous penitentiary in Britain. They just believe nobody would ever dare attempt what we're going to do. It's just not on, old boy.'

He picked up a cardboard cylinder he'd brought with him and extracted from it a rolled-up sheet of draughtman's paper, which he spread out on the table and anchored at each corner with improvised paperweights. It was a detailed plan of 'D' Hall in Wormwood Scrubs, the central prison or Top Security Wing for long-term dangerous prisoners and habitual escapers. It ran from north to south a hundred and twenty yards long and twenty-five yards distance from the East boundary wall. On each of the two long sides of the building were the cells; on the two shorter sides were workshops, store-rooms, the offices of prison staff and the recreation halls. The large barred windows looked out on the prison yard where the marked dimensions showed it was a distance of seventy-five feet to the outer perimeter stone walls, with a high fence of wire mesh intervening.

'See this?' said Carrington as the three

men pored over the plan. 'This is the way out, this landing on the second floor with its large window over the entrance hall. X marks the spot. The cast iron bars over it have been there since the Flood and never renewed. Every layer of rust has been painted over with smart black paint until the bars are just layer cakes of rust and paint. A couple of strokes with a hacksaw and they can be kicked right out. There's a distance of twenty-two feet from there to the ground, but the drop is really only half that because the clever duffers have built a covered way right under the window, so that the escaper can lower himself on to it without much of a jolt at all. The second stage of the drop is even easier because they've stuck a large refuse bin with a wooden top at the end of the covered way. Once he's down on that it's only five feet to the ground.'

'Well, how about that?' breathed Bradley Chawton. 'It's unbelievable! Just imagine 'em having prisoners' aids like that at San Quentin or Attica or Leavenworth!'

24

'Here, slow down a bit,' growled Haldane. 'You talk as if there's nobody but this Gingerman in the whole bloody prison. What are the screws going to be doing while he's filing through a set of bars, smashing his way through a window and making two jumps down to the ground?'

'Oh, that's been thought through and the prison procedure's been well vetted. On Saturday evening at 5 pm all the cons locked inside 'D' Hall are on free association for two hours. That means they can stroll through the landings, watch TV, play chess or ping-pong if they're intellectuals, wander in and out of one another's cells, or just stand about in groups talking. Most of 'em go into a film show with a couple of screws, and as everybody's relaxed in a happy mood there's generally only two more screws on duty in 'D' Hall to mind all the rest. Nobody need see a thing when he goes through that second-floor landing window.'

'OK, OK,' said Haldane. 'So he's down on the ground outside 'D' Hall.

How does he get through the wire mesh fence to the perimeter wall, and up over it through the barbed-wire entanglement on top? What about the patrolling screws and guard dogs, and the closed-circuit TV monitors that are stuck up on poles at intervals along the wire mesh fence and the main stone wall?'

'The perimeter patrol has been carefully timed,' replied Carrington. 'It takes him exactly eight minutes to do the round of the prison wall. And there's a back-up officer in a small shed near the main gate with a telephone to the orderly office. He generally smokes or reads a comic or has a snooze till his watch is over, bored to tears, so he's not likely to notice anything. The patrolling guards change over at half-past the hour and always spend some time yakking together with no sense of urgency: our old friend the English Disease again. So we can be practically certain that the perimeter patrol won't come walking by on the stroke of half-past. The Gingerman will be supplied with a quartz digital watch so that he can time his break-out from

'D' Hall with split-second accuracy. Once he's down it's only a matter of seconds to run along the covered way and reach the wire mesh fence. The bought screw inside the prison will also have smuggled him in some powerful bolt cutters which he'll use to hack a quick way through the wire mesh. Once through there he's at the perimeter wall.

'At a pre-arranged time, six-thirty to the second, with the aid of another quartz digital, a big furniture van will come down the narrow lane into Artillery Road and stop up against the prison wall. A red cross will have been painted on the wall a minute before to tell the driver the exact spot to place the van. Then the driver gets up on the roof, puts a lightweight ladder up to the wall and cuts through the barbed-wire entanglement with his own bolt cutters. Then he flings over the wall a rope ladder made of nylon thread, each rung reinforced by a steel knitting needle which holds the rungs taut and makes climbing more easy. The Gingerman by this time is right underneath waiting for it. He hauls himself up fast and drops on the roof of the pantechnicon, pulling the nylon ladder up behind him.

'In the few seconds that this has been going on our highly paid technical man who's been bought on the inside has shorted out the main capacitor on the TV monitor, so that there's only a blurred distortion and no picture at all on the screens of what's being done along the perimeter wall. The screw on watch fiddles about with his switches and thumps the box a few times the way ignoramuses always do when their telly goes on the blink. Then after a minute and a half flat, which is all that's needed for the Gingerman to cut through the mesh and be over the wall and away, the capacitor is switched back in again and the screw on watch is happy, thinking that his thumping on the box has fixed it. With all that going smoothly there can't be more than a few minutes before the alarm will be raised. The perimeter patrol will come by and is bound to notice the hole that's been cut in the wire mesh fence. But by then the Gingerman will have been transferred from the pantechnicon to a fast car and whisked away to the pick-up point, where he'll be put on his way to the boondocks.

'As you can see the success of the operation depends on a rigid, prearranged time schedule with a margin of only a few seconds either way. With quartz technology it's possible, provided the Gingerman memorises his programme and his movements are perfectly synchronised with those of the men on the other side of the wall. What do you think?'

'Well, it's certainly got style,' admitted Chawton. 'Given the usual British inefficiency in security matters I think it could just about work. Yes, I like it. It's just zany enough to come off.'

'I'm not sold on it,' declared Haldane flatly. 'There are too many things left to chance. What if another lousy con spots our man filing through the bars and insists on breaking out with him? What if the English Disease isn't active for once, and the perimeter patrol with his dog happens to be walking past the spot just as the nylon ladder comes flying over?'

'That's the grey area we can do nothing about,' shrugged Carrington.

'Then there's that big if with the TV monitor. How can you be sure your technician will be able to work on that capacitor for the vital minute without being spotted by the screw on watch?'

'Oh, come on,' said Carrington impatiently. 'We're springing a man from a top security gaol, not organising a bloody two-car funeral. There have to be risks in this. All I know is that there's a senior screw been bought inside the Scrubs, and he'll see to it that the Gingerman gets his digital watch, hacksaw blade, bolt-cutters and the necessary briefing. Make your choice. It's either the Gingerman who we know we can trust security-wise as well as with the test tubes, or it's scouring the dregs for some bent little production chemist with no bottle, who's probably out of a job through incompetence and who'll sell us out to the fuzz if things get a bit hairy.'

'So when do we give these Houdinis the go-ahead?' said Chawton, rubbing his hands gleefully. 'What date did you have in mind as Liberation Day for the Gingerman?'

'It can't be till we get vacant possession of the farm and Hal's moved in,' said Carrington. 'So we may as well leave the Gingerman on ice to be taken care of in the Scrubs until we've got somewhere safe for him to live and work. We can't just have him running about loose and getting put back in the slammer after we've paid twenty grand for him.'

'This farm,' said Haldane. 'It's definitely available? You've got a half-nelson on the owner?'

'You can depend on it,' Carrington assured him. 'It's a hundred per cent certain he'll come through for us. He's one of these people afflicted from birth by the English Disease I was telling you about, a terminal case. It's always a lot of laughs to prick their bubble and hear them howl.'

3

Digby Mackworth Uteric Carvell of Eton, Cambridge and the Guards, Member of Parliament, junior minister in the Home Office at 38, was a young Adonis who had it all: media support and hero worship, Prime Ministerial approval, grass roots adulation. Tall and slim with a handsome patrician face and a crop of wavy auburn hair which tended to fall forward over his brow in a poetic wave as he thundered passionately at the rostrum, he was a compelling and charismatic speaker. His powerful flowing oratory always grabbed the hearts and minds of the party faithful, establishing his claim on them as the future custodian of party ideals and philosophy. Indeed he was strongly tipped as a future Home Secretary when the present dithering, jaded and lack-lustre holder of that office was eventually removed.

Digby's star quality was well matched

by his inordinate political ambition. From his father, a millionaire merchant banker, he'd inherited an estate in Northamptonshire, five thousand rolling acres comprising forty-two tenant farms, which he contrived to run as a tax loss to offset his swingeing tax liability from City interests.

One of Digby's more brilliant strokes was his marriage to a Duke's daughter, thereby securing his flank against the machinations of a corrupt, cruel and whimsical Establishment. It also ensured that the best houses in London were open to him for the high spots of the social calendar. His wife Lucinda preferred to stay for most of the year at their country seat of Aldingbourne Manor with her two young daughters, Emma and Jane, and her numerous horses and dogs with which she'd always been at ease. She found London Society terribly fraught and the mandatory social whirl a frightful bore, while Digby's constant high-powered political endeavours gave her a headache.

So Digby lived at the town house, a

first-floor luxury apartment in a purpose-built mansion block in Park Lane called Hamilton Towers. Here, barely a mile from his magisterial room in the Home Office in Queen Anne's Gate, Digby lived a life of bachelor freedom, surrounded by his own lovely things, able to entertain his own guests and pursue his own social round in his capacity as a well born and impeccably connected minister of the Crown. He was also able to indulge freely his Number Two passion which was lifting skirts. He was a career politician first and a hedonist second, as pushy in grabbing his pleasures as a horny travelling salesman. To his closest friends and some enemies who'd rumbled him he was the House of Commons Groper.

'A pity about the dear boy's frantic womanising,' said his friends. 'If the PM ever gets to know of his little habits, his return to the back benches could be electrifying. And if it ever leaks out to the prurient masses it could cost him some crucial votes at the coming election.'

But Digby was sharp and discreet in

34

his social gamesmanship. He chose the beautiful, well endowed and experienced divorcees with no troublesome proprietorial male in their lives, or the idle, bored young wife of some foreign diplomat or visiting trade official who was very much a bird of passage. He ensured that he got the bedroom antics and physical titillation without any emotional involvement complicating his life. It had always worked infallibly for him until he became involved with Elaine Cornford, but he lost control of that situation because he was in love. Elaine worked a unique and devastating intoxication on him so that he found himself — experienced fancier though he was — in over his head before he realised what had hit him.

They met at a brilliant reception at the French Embassy, where Digby first discovered that Elaine was launched on Society as a fashionable portrait painter. It was *de rigueur* to the trendsetters to have their portrait painted by Elaine Cornford. Inevitably she painted Digby's portrait in his Number One dress uniform as a lieutenant in the Grenadier Guards, looking pensively patriotic and charismatic against the natural and dignified setting of his great drawing-room window which looked out on the formal, regimented greenery of Hyde Park, the Serpentine and Kensington Gardens.

Elaine was a slender ethereal creature, as fragile looking as a geisha girl, and tended to flutter gracefully in all her movements. She had a pale oval face and huge dark eyes which seemed to glow with passionate innocence. Her thick dark brown hair grew half-way down her back and was secured with a gold clasp in a kind of voluptuous pony tail. She dressed in loose flowing gowns and shifts which always contrived to show a teasing outline of her exquisitely moulded form. Men of all ages, colours and conditions were drawn to her like wasps to a honey-pot, so she could afford to be very choosey.

Accustomed to the instant admiration of the rich and famous, she chose Digby because of his aristocratic connections, his wealth and political status. Power to her was an aphrodisiac.

Her own background and origins were a closely guarded secret, for they were undistinguished if not actually seedy. She was the second daughter of a small town station master in the West Midlands, and had been educated at the neighbourhood comprehensive school until she discovered her flair for painting and left at sixteen to go to Art College.

After a wild and riotous year in London she went to live with a Frenchman in Paris, and supported him by sketching ten-minute crayon portraits of the free-spending foreign tourists on the pavements of Montmartre. Having survived some years of a turbulent, precarious and somewhat depraved Bohemian existence, she decided to return to London and settle down to make her way as a serious painter.

In order to commercialise her gift she married an art dealer and general promoter called Donald Carrington, who operated on the outskirts of fraud in the vast twilight area of London's fine arts exchange. It was Carrington's shrewd perception and energetic salesmanship that first launched Elaine as a successful commercial painter. But before he could cash in on her success he landed in gaol for planting a counterfeit old master on an Arab, and Elaine learnt to manage very well without him.

Digby knew vaguely that Elaine had a husband somewhere — which pretty woman past her teens did not? — but he thought it was just a shallow meaningless relationship, carelessly entered into in a moment of her giddy youth and soon forgotten; an embarrassing entanglement she was keen to disavow now that she was rich and famous in her own right. Besotted though he was with Elaine, Digby was enough of a pragmatist and shrewd political survivor to have dropped her and run from such a minefield, if only he'd known she was still under the domination of an ex-convict who was a most ingenious and versatile villain.

★ ★ ★

Digby had temporarily escaped from his onerous duties at Queen Anne's Gate, delegating various chores to the vortex of earnest-faced sycophants that whirled around him, and was preparing himself for an afternoon session with Elaine. With Denim Aftershave liberally applied round his cheeks and jowls, Leather and Old Spice in his armpits, and his pecker generously anointed with Patchouli, Digby was a walking mélange of the most seductive smells.

He paid off his taxi in Chelsea at the top of Flood Street, and walked rather furtively to Elaine's elegant three-storey house. Elaine admitted him and took him immediately upstairs to her richly furnished and deliciously perfumed boudoir.

She was dressed only in a long, flowing diaphanous white gown like some goddess of classical antiquity, so that when she stood with the light behind her, as she contrived to do fairly frequently, Digby could see the clear outline of her exquisite nudity. She wore no underclothes at all. His breathing quickened and his blood pressure rose with all the demanding urgency of a lustful young stud, but Elaine had him so well trained that he just sat riveted on the Victorian *chaise longue* before her, silently worshipping in his pain.

It was sternly forbidden to him even to speak of sex until she gave him a certain signal. If he incurred her displeasure by anything so gross as attempted pawing and kissing before she was ready, she was likely to banish him from her favours for a week or more with the haughty, wounding distaste of a goddess. Part of the reason why she held him so much in thrall was that he'd never been able to establish any kind of ascendancy over her. He was no more sure of her now than he'd been in the early agonising days of his courtship when she'd strung him along with such anguished uncertainty as to whether she'd ever go to bed with him or not. But once she'd decided to take him on she astounded him with such a wealth of creative depravity, such passionate genius for the sexual arts that Digby knew she was unique. Nobody else he'd ever met in all his vast experience could match her.

She'd always made it clear that she was the dominant partner, that everything depended on her mood, on her feelings and appetites of the moment. She was a new generation feminist. When she made love it was entirely for her own greedy pleasure, and the man of the hour was only her instrument. On one occasion, to show her steel-like supremacy, she'd made Digby lie beside her all night in bed while she was insulated from him by a flimsy nylon night dress which she stubbornly and wilfully refused to take off. The knowledge was implicit that if he'd tried to force her in his raging need, their relationship would have been terminated abruptly. She would never speak to him again. Like a hungry but well trained dog he had to wait for the crook of a finger, the swing of a hip, or a certain sparkle in her eye that told him it was all right to come bounding up, fawning and slobbering all over her for the ultimate glory of possession.

When she suddenly suggested that

they spend a few stolen days together in her seaside house at Brighton, an amenity which Digby never even knew she possessed till now, his simmering desire blazed up at fever heat at the ecstatic promise underlying the offer. He foresaw difficulties to be circumvented of course. He was much in demand along the path of duty. He'd been landed with the awful job of trying to convince the Police Federation in a major speech why they must tighten up the control and issue of firearms to their members when there wasn't a cat in hell's chance of the Death Penalty being reintroduced to protect policemen against the gun-carrying classes. The Home Office was getting a very bad press these days, mainly due to the waffling, bumbling incompetence of its chief executive, who was managing to attract a lot of flak even from the Party faithful. Please God the tedious old duffer would soon fall under a bus, so that Digby could come into his own.

'Darling, please say you'll come,' pleaded Elaine. 'I hate going away on my own, but I feel I really must get out of London for a bit. If I don't soon get some clean sea air and an easing of all the social pressures, I shall explode. Brighton is home from home to me. I got to love it when I was a girl at Roedean. Mummy and Daddy used to come at the weekend to take me out for afternoon tea.'

'Of course I'd be absolutely delighted to spend a holiday with you in Brighton or anywhere else,' said Digby eagerly.

'Good. It's agreed then. We'll travel down together tomorrow on the train from Victoria.'

Digby's face fell a mile as the self-preserving politician in him surfaced to take control.

'Oh dear, I'm afraid that might not be easy to arrange, darling,' he said hastily. 'There's so much to be done at the office that absolutely needs my control and signature. I really can't give a firm time for catching any train. Why don't you go on ahead, and I'll follow in the next day or two.'

'Ashamed to be seen with me on public transport?' she chided him gently. 'My word, what a hypocritical, career-hungry prig you are, Digby!'

'Not at all,' he retorted with a snooty look. 'When one's a public servant one has to accept the responsibilities that go with the office. Dropping everything to rush away on holiday at a moment's notice is just not on.'

'You work much too hard in your beastly government office,' declared Elaine fiercely. 'Why kill yourself at some rotten bureaucratic job when you don't need to?'

'Why indeed!' said Digby smugly. 'One can only explain it in terms of something greater than oneself, a feeling of walking with Destiny perhaps.'

'Come here, you pompous idiot,' said Elaine softly with a sparkle of sultry sexual complicity in her eye. 'I bet I can make you forget your lofty Destiny in thirty seconds flat.'

His eager boyish heart bounded with a surge of joy so deliciously intense as to become a pain as he succumbed to her.

4

The following day by late afternoon Digby had tidied up in his department and delegated all immediate problems for handling or shelving to his permanent private secretary. He sneaked out of London in the rush hour driving the anonymous Japanese car he kept for such top security forays.

In some respects being a famous and photogenic minister was as disadvantageous as being a fugitive. Anything as suggestive as a distinguished politician sneaking off to Brighton alone would inevitably invite malicious speculation and comment, which in turn could arouse the prurient interest of investigative journalists, that scourge of the great and gifted! Once those swine caught a whiff of the slightest scandal, Digby's hero-worshipped image was as good as smashed for ever.

A swift, pleasant and uneventful run

brought him to the outskirts of Brighton, and then it was just a case of rolling downhill to the busy and picturesque esplanade. Elaine's seaside house lay back in a smart Regency terrace in a dignified square of lawns and colourful flower-beds within sight of the open sea. Digby was impressed as much by her impeccable taste as by her considerable financial resources that made possession of such a property possible, considering it was merely a holiday home and must remain unoccupied for most of the year.

As he climbed out of the car and started to haul his two suitcases through the rear hatch, the front door of Elaine's house opened and she came out to greet him. She was dressed as usual in one of her long flowing gowns with a disturbing degree of transparency, and her thick brown hair flowed unrestrained about her shoulders with a delicious suggestion of abandonment and intimacy.

'Hullo darling,' she said softly, giving him a chaste peck on the cheek. 'I'm so glad you could come. You're in plenty of time for dinner. It's only a lobster salad, I'm afraid — one tends to live on salads and sea food at the seaside — but awfully good for one's calorie control and complexion. Come along inside and I'll show you to your room.'

Digby felt vaguely irritated at the words 'your room' and not 'our room', just as if she intended him to sleep chastely in his own bed like a maiden aunt. Had she brought him down here just to put him through all that sadistic teasing ritual again? They walked up the stone steps to the pillared portico, Digby puffing slightly from the unaccustomed exertion of carrying his own suitcases.

Inside the square entrance hall with its Italian terrazzo floor and panelled walls there was an old-fashioned Victorian hatstand with a man's off-white belted raincoat and soft brown trilby hat prominently displayed there. Digby stiffened with jealous anger and a sudden premonition of alarm, his first icy shock of wounding suspicion that the delectable Elaine wasn't all he'd thought her to be.

'Elaine!' he hissed accusingly. 'Who

does that hat and coat belong to? My God! You've not got another man here, have you?'

'Come along darling,' she said serenely. 'Leave your luggage at the foot of the stairs for now and let's go in the lounge. There's someone I'd like you to meet.'

She took his hand while he was still too shaken to resist and pulled him somewhat precipitately through a panelled doorway into a large sitting room, opulently furnished with modern upholstered chairs and settees, and draped with rich matching fabrics.

Standing at a bow-fronted window gazing pensively out on to the lawns and gardens and wooden seats round the square was a squat, swarthy, black-haired man with a slightly pitted face, dressed for the summer in casual slacks and an open-necked shirt with brightly coloured cravat. He was about the same age as Digby, but there all resemblance ended. In contrast with Digby's elegant lissom figure and finely chiselled handsomeness, the other man was positively repulsive; a man who would curse and brawl and let the side down with the most reprehensible lack of breeding. Even though Digby never had to associate with low-living ruffians he knew instinctively that this man was at best some kind of a shifty tradesman in dealing with whom one would always get the worst of any bargain.

'Darling,' said Elaine sweetly, 'this is my friend from the Home Office I've been telling you about, Mr Digby Carvell. Digby, this is my husband, Donald Carrington.'

'Husband!' gasped Digby, almost petrified with horror.

'Pleased to meet you, Digby, old boy,' said the other in a resonant, powerful voice with no distinguishable accent. 'A friend of the family, are you?' And he laughed a booming, hearty laugh in which there was neither mirth nor sincerity.

Digby limply took the proffered hand, broad, stubby-fingered, hirsute and powerful, and tried to recover his badly shaken self-possession.

'Mr Carrington,' he said lamely, 'you have me at a disadvantage. I never knew

Elaine had a husband.'

Carrington's unpleasant laugh rang out again, and Elaine said reproachfully:

'Oh Digby, I told you the first time we ever met that I was spoken for.'

'And as I remember,' said Digby with growing resentment, 'you also said you were alone and independent, a career girl first and foremost. I naturally assumed your marriage was an unsatisfactory brief experiment, finished and forgotten, as with so many militant feminists who refuse to be anybody's slave and chattel. Damnit, you told me often enough that you'd never be anybody's little woman.'

'Oh no,' replied Elaine. 'You assumed too much, and it was all wishful thinking. But as the illusion seemed to make you so happy I was too soft-hearted to disillusion you. Donald and I are still very much married, even though we go our separate ways careerwise. It just happens that Donald has been out of the country on business for the last two years, but we always keep in touch.'

'Well, good Lord, you might have told me he'd be here in Brighton, instead of just pitching me unexpectedly into this compromising situation. Haven't you any idea of the embarrassment? I mean, what sort of a fool it makes me look?'

'Nonsense, dear boy. Relax,' said Elaine soothingly. 'How can you possibly feel embarrassed among friends who love you? If you think Donald has any crude possessive jealously over me, you're completely mistaken. Isn't that so, Donald?'

'Absolutely. None of that old-fashioned nonsense about us. I trust Elaine's judgment and she trusts mine. Any friend of Elaine can depend on me right up to the hilt. Here, let me get you a drink, old boy.'

He crossed the room to a carved oak sideboard on which stood a large array of bottles, and poured Digby a generous helping of Scotch in a tumbler.

'Sorry there's no ice,' he said. 'Elaine forgot to switch the fridge on when she got here and it's not cooked yet. I'm only just back from the States myself, and I miss the technology like hell.'

'Dinner in a quarter of an hour, boys,'

said Elaine briskly. 'I'll have to leave you two together for a bit. I'm sure you've got lots to talk about.'

As she glided out of the room like a shimmering wraith the two men warily appraised each other, and Digby grew even more uneasy. He realised already that Elaine had lured him neatly into some kind of a trap. Every room in the bloody house was probably bugged three different ways. He knew that as a public figure in the modest echelons of government he was always highly vulnerable to the scandal created by some dirty, media-inspired ambush. And now here he was in this house, set up in a highly dubious threesome with a devious, inscrutable bitch and her unscrupulous husband. He could only wait with growing trepidation for the unveiling of the bottom line: how much was it going to cost him to get out of this well-sprung trap?

On a sudden angry impulse he decided to bring everything straight out into the open.

'Was it your idea to invite me down

here into this absurd situation?' he demanded bluntly. 'Does it appeal to your perverse sense of humour, or is there some other motive behind it?'

'Since you ask,' retorted Carrington coolly, 'I always like to run the rule over my wife's friends, to keep a protective eye on her, so to speak, while I'm away on business. Elaine is a very sweet and generous girl, but the world being what it is, there are freaks and adventurers everywhere who could give her a very bad time if she hadn't got somebody like me looking out for her. When she told me about you I was very impressed. I wanted to meet you, so I told her to invite you down here where the social and professional demands on you can't intrude.'

'And that's really all?' said Digby hopefully.

'Well, since we're indulging in a cards-on-the-table session, Digby old boy, it had occurred to me that you might be a useful chap to know. With ministerial rank in the Home Office you must have a lot of clout. As for me, I reckon nobody in this life is so strong and self-sufficient that there won't come a day when he could use a discreet helping hand from a man at the Ministry.'

Digby went cold with shocked dismay, and sweat broke out all over him as his quick mind grasped the implication.

'Don't be absurd,' he blustered. 'I can't help you in any way in my capacity as minister. I wouldn't even if I could. This is not America, you know. There are high standards of rectitude and probity in British public life, and when a minister feels unable to live up to them he invariably resigns.'

Carrington greeted the end of this speech with a slow, solemn handclap, so that Digby became more flustered, and felt himself a bigger prick than ever.

'Relax. Wind down, Digby old boy,' said Carrington soothingly. 'Here, let me top your glass up. Elaine tells me you're a very able and ambitious politician, that you have a great future ahead of you. In fact you've set your sights on the Top Table, and with your background and everything going for you, I'd put money on you getting there. Unless of course you foul it up by some shocking scandal. Let's face it, Digby old boy, you are rather a glutton for putting your hands on other men's women, aren't you? Although it may not mean much to the average guy nowadays who's screwing who, I don't somehow think they'll have you at the Top Table if it's known to the electorate that you're a hard playing, indiscriminate cocksman. Lloyd George got away with it just, because the news media of his day were so primitive, and by the time it did leak out his career was over. But things are different now. They'll crucify you for a Roman holiday, Digby old boy, and your closest friends and colleagues will rejoice the loudest.'

'I won't be blackmailed!' exclaimed Digby furiously. 'I'd rather resign and go to the back benches.'

'No you wouldn't,' replied Carrington smoothly. 'It's all true that power is an addictive drug as well as an aphrodisiac. Anybody who's once had it is well and truly hooked for life. Giving it all up is a kind of death. Living would be empty and meaningless to you, Digby old boy, exiled from the Westminster scene, striding over your God-forsaken acres in Northamptonshire or wherever with straw in your hair. Besides, there's no need to give it all up on my account. I'm not going to blackmail you.'

'Then why are we having this conversation?' demanded Digby tensely. 'What exactly did you mean by a helping hand from a man at the Ministry?'

'Well, it so happens I'm a pushover for helping lame dogs,' said Carrington unctuously. 'Never could turn aside from a poor bastard down on his luck. There's this old friend of mine, you see, Henry Haldane just back from Rhodesia. It sounds like a good place to leave from now that the black commies have taken it over. Hal had a ten thousand acre farm that his great grandfather hacked out of the bush and built up with his own bare hands. Hal wanted to stay there where he was born, and take his chance with the new régime, but law and order is breaking down fast.

There are these marauding gangs of black bandits ranging all over the countryside with their Russian-made Kalatchnikovs, shooting up the homesteads, driving off the cattle, murdering the white farmers and their women and children. Hal had such a close call when they ambushed his Jeep on a country road that he decided to get out while he was still in one piece, even though he was only allowed to bring a miserable three-hundred quid out with him. He'd like to get started farming in this country — it's the only job he knows — but he hasn't got the capital, not even for two acres and a cow. So that's where you come in, Digby old boy, with your *noblesse oblige.*'

'Me!' choked Digby, feeling he was going into shock again. 'What can I do for him?'

'Oh come on, Digby. I know all about your country seat at Aldingbourne Manor in Northamptonshire, your five thousand acres and forty-two tenant farms that you run as a tax loss against your City fiddles. Because of the low rents you charge them all your tenant farmers think you're Jesus and Father Christmas. God bless you, Squire!'

'I can't help you,' said Digby flatly. 'All the tenancies are taken. In any case my estate manager deals with the re-letting. I'm far too busy at Westminster to worry about domestic problems.'

'Ah yes, your estate manager, Mr Alvin Ballsover who lives at The Lodge. I had quite an interesting chat with him a week ago in the village pub at Aldingbourne. The Lord Burleigh, isn't it? I got talking to him over drinks about farms to let in the neighbourhood, and he mentioned that place on the outer edge of your estate, Woodfield Hollow, that's coming vacant in September. A hundred acres of prime land, a cosy farmhouse of Colly Weston stone, a good spread of outbuildings. He's a shrewd, down-to-earth fellow, your Alvin Ballsover. He drives a hard bargain with his talk about a year's rent in advance, and payment for stock and equipement at valuation.'

Digby stared at him in shocked incredulity.

'You mean you've actually been

snooping about my property up there, questioning my estate manager?'

'Ballsover told me all about the Pyke family at Woodfield Hollow,' went on Carrington cheerfully, 'how they're clearing out in August to go farming in New Zealand because they can't take all the interference from Brussels. Alvin's promised the vacant tenancy to an old friend of his, but I'm sure you could over-rule that bit of favouritism with your owner's prerogative. That farm is just right for poor old Henry Haldane, and he'd work the land into tip-top condition for you. There's no farmer as good as a hungry farmer.'

'I make it a rule never to interfere with Mr Ballsover's running of the estate,' said Digby with stubborn desperation. 'If the tenancy is promised, I'd never ask Ballsover to go back on his word. Your friend from Rhodesia can find plenty of other suitable tenant farms if he cares to stir himself and look around.'

'Digby old boy,' said Carrington, shaking his head at him sadly, 'I don't think you're hearing me or getting the picture, so I'll have to talk to you like a Dutch uncle. Even though the old institution of marriage is degraded to nothing these days, there's still legal divorce, and they still use that quaint old word, co-respondent. For an ordinary guy to be cited as co-respondent may not mean much. But with you, Digby, the PM's blue-eyed boy, set for the giddy heights, just think what the media could make of that. Your romance with Elaine would become a *cause célèbre* overnight, and then goodbye to the Top Table. Medusa the Gorgon at Number Ten, the knacker-cracker who turns men to stone with a single glance, would chop you right off at the short hairs and flush you down the sewer.'

Digby winced and shuddered and cringed inwardly at this graphic pronunciation of a doom which he couldn't even bear to contemplate. He wanted to break away from Carrington and that hellish room and run and never stop running. What the hell was he doing here? But a nightmare power held him rooted to his seat.

'I'll speak to Ballsover,' he muttered. 'The tenancy isn't really his to dispose of. There's no reason why it shouldn't be offered to my nominee.'

'Splendid,' said Carrington warmly. 'I knew you'd come through for us, Digby. You've no idea how big a favour you'll be doing for a poor devil hounded out of his own country and forced to leave everything behind. And while we're on the subject of poor old Henry Haldane, if he's going to run a farm here he needs Home Office permission to stay. At present he's being treated like an enemy alien and given a temporary entry visa for eight days. It might be renewed. It probably won't be because he's a member of a despised race. We all know how trendy officialdom has to show its continuing love for our black brothers by cracking down hard on the evil white racists who've been maltreating them all these years. Haldane needs a resident's permit valid for a year and subject to renewal until he can be naturalised. I'm sure you wouldn't mind helping things along at the Immigration and

Aliens Department. With your clout you could easily over-ride the shiny-arsed desk warriors who like to make everybody sweat.'

'You don't know what you're asking,' exclaimed Digby vehemently. 'It's quite out of the question. There are other people involved in the immigration process. It would be noticed immediately if I interfered. Why should I be forced out of office in a scandal of corruption through giving favoured status to your unsavoury friend?'

'I seem to remember you interfered in the case of that Polish seaman who jumped ship in London,' said Carrington harshly. 'You soon bundled him off back to the Gulag Archipelago. He's probably taken a dive through the tenth floor window of a psychiatric hospital by now. Then there's that murdering black bastard over here from Zimbabwe. You gave him a resident's permit without getting involved in a scandal of corruption, didn't you? So why be so prissy about stretching a point for poor old Henry Haldane who's at his wits' end, facing certain death if they deport him back to that shambles. Isn't there a ministerial reshuffle in the offing about now?'

'Dinner is served, boys,' trilled Elaine, shimmering into the room. 'Come along. Digby, you look positively faint with hunger. Darling, will you deal with the wine?'

5

On a damp misty Saturday night in October the plan to free the Gingerman was put into operation. Terence George Munton, known in the underworld as the Gingerman because of his pale sandy hair, matching eyebrows and drooping ginger moustache was whisked over the high wall of Wormwood Scrubs, with only one dicey moment. On climbing the nylon ladder to the top of the wall, he was caught up in the barbed wire entanglement surmounting it. He was barely dragged clear in time by the escapologist from the pantechnicon who'd cut a jagged way through the wire. As it was, Munton's Prison suit was ripped to shreds and he had painful gashes on his arms and backside. With seconds to spare, according to the tight time schedule, the capacitor on the TV monitor was wired back in service, and the long perspective view of the prison wall came back on the screens.

Three minutes later the perimeter patrol came striding past with his dog and spotted the neat aperture which had been cut in the wire mesh fence by Terry Munton. Instantly the alarm was raised, the sirens blared angrily, all the other gleeful convicts were herded back to their cells, and police cars zeroed in from all sides on Shepherd's Bush to set up road-blocks on all roads leading away from the prison. But by this time the Gingerman had been transferred from the pantechnicon to a waiting car, which had whirled him well clear of the area to his rendezvous with Henry Haldane.

Munton's escape caused an immediate national outcry, a massive inquisition into prison security, and a vigorous clamp-down on all privileges available to the inmates. Two officers were suspended from duty and exhaustively interrogated by Scotland Yard detectives, for Terence Munton had earned his status as a Category 'A' prisoner. Not only was he an illegal drugs manufacturer and distributor on a massive scale. He was also an ingenious Houdini who'd escaped successfully from several lesser prisons during his long career in crime.

A chemistry graduate and research worker of Queen Mary College, Munton had soon discovered that lawfully earned salaries were derisory compared with the profits from amphetamines, barbiturates and hallucinogenics which he could manufacture for the alternative society. Despite his several convictions and custodial sentences Munton always went back to it, a hardened and incorrigible expansionist of drugs abuse.

In appearance Munton was short, slightly built and wiry, with a thin pointed face like a rodent's, and disarmingly soft brown eyes with the permanently ingratiating expression of a vote-seeking politician or a priest on the make with his choir boys. He was only into the second year of his ten-year stretch, so it came to him like an unbelievable gift from the gods when he was informed by the screw liaison in Wormwood Scrubs that a London firm was paying big money to have him sprung so that they could cash in on his notorious skills.

As he drove north with Haldane on the M1 the Rhodesian briefed him on why he'd been sprung, where he was going for refuge, and the terms of his employment.

'We've laid out a lot of money to get you out of that bloody cage, Munton,' said Haldane bluntly, 'so you'd better be worth it.'

'Oh I'm more than worth it, chief,' said the Gingerman with due servility. 'Mass producing lsd microdots is child's play. I can do 'em in my sleep by the thousand. You want phenyl acetic acid (Speed) or diethylpropion hydrochloride (Blueys), or Angel Dust, I can do that too. If you want the big H, just get me the gear.'

'Your mug is going to be on every newspaper and TV screen in the country by this time tomorrow,' went on Haldane ignoring his offer. 'You'll be billed as the Gingerman, so you're going to stay close on my farm, grow a beard and dye your hair, eyebrows and whiskers black before you even walk across a field.'

'Christ, guv'nor, I don't much like the sound of that,' grumbled Munton. 'I don't think much of the rural life either, and I don't reckon the countryside is the safest place to put down a lab. It's easier to lose it in the middle of a town with all the other factories and workshops and spare accommodation, and all the comings and goings round about.'

'We didn't spring you to talk about the grand strategy,' retorted Haldane coldly. 'You're being paid and well paid to look after the production side of the operation, because we got good references on your work record and character. But if you'd rather be back in that stinking zoo, playing with yourself till you grow old and rot . . . '

'Oh no, chief. Not bloody likely,' interposed Munton hastily. 'I owe you for getting me out of there. I'm never going back. I'll grow hair all over and live up a sodding tree if you say so.'

Munton had already taken stock of the sunburnt Selous Scout with his cold, piercing eyes and harsh Rhodesian accent, and decided he was a real hard man, one to go along with rather than mess about. If he did have any soft spots Munton would suss them quickly enough and know how to exploit them to his own advantage.

When they reached Kettering it was barely nine o'clock, but the streets were virtually deserted in the thin drizzle that was falling.

'Jesus wept!' grumbled Haldane. 'This dump must be the only cemetery in the world with traffic lights.'

He pulled into the car park of a large pub and bought a couple of bottles of whisky and a dozen cans of ale.

'By way of a welcome home party to Woodfield Hollow,' he explained nonchalantly. 'As you're not allowed out on the town, the least we can do is wet your whistle behind closed doors.'

A few more miles out into the country and they arrived at Woodfield Hollow, which lay about a mile off the main road along a narrow lane leading to a village. As they drove into the dark farmyard Munton saw his future home lit up by the car's headlights. It was a low, rambling, two-storey building of local stone, with a roof of thick stone slabs and small, picturesque, diamond-paned windows. Nearby was the cluster of barns, sheds and other typical farm buildings, pride of place being taken by a new long low factory-like shed of modern prefabricated concrete. This had been designed as a modern milking parlour and dairy, but was now fitted out with all the chemical equipment needed for the manufacture of lsd.

The first thing Munton heard as he got out of the car was the deep baying of a big dog coming from the farmhouse, a savage and menacing sound which chilled the blood.

'That's Angus, my Doberman,' said Haldane casually. 'Any nosey bugger who comes snooping round here will get more than he bargained for. Angus answers to me and nobody else.'

'What about me?' said Munton apprehensively. 'How can I do my job here if I'm pinned down at every move by a bloody great hound?'

'Don't worry. He won't have you unless

I tell him to. The important thing is not to make any quick or sudden moves. Above all, try not to show fear. That turns him on.'

Inside the farmhouse whose walls were three feet thick the beamed ceilings were low and the rooms were large and rambling. In the living room there was a huge stone fireplace built from grey slabs of the local Colly Weston stone. It would hold a fire big enough to roast an ox and keep the building from freezing up in the bitterest winter.

Haldane had already taken the biggest and most comfortable bedroom for himself. He allocated Munton to a smaller and drabber room over the farm kitchen. It contained a single old-fashioned brass bedstead equipped with a stained old flock mattress and some coarse army blankets. There was a battered old wardrobe with the veneer peeling off, a chest of drawers and a strip of threadbare carpet on the varnished boards. The walls were newly whitewashed, and there was a framed tapestry hanging over the bed with the embroidered text:

'How short is life's uncertain race, Alas! How quickly run . . .'

'Well, I suppose it's better than my peter on 'D' Hall, just about,' said Munton resignedly. 'Don't you have any sheets for the bed, guv'nor?'

'What for?' said Haldane brusquely. 'I didn't think you'd know what they were for.'

'Oh come on, guv. I'm an ordinary respectable con, not an old tattooed lag from Devil's Island who keeps his money up his arse. Isn't there anybody else going to be living here apart from you and me and that bloody wolf?'

'What do you think!'

'No cosy little woman to do the cooking and cleaning and take care of the home comforts?'

'And blab her mouth off about what we're making here,' said Haldane contemptuously. 'Don't be bloody stupid.'

'I'm not sure I like this arrangement, living here with you like a couple of poofs.'

'Don't worry. You're not my type,'

said Haldane grimly. 'And it can't be as bad here as being banged up in an eight-by-six cell with some creep who's permanently crazy for an orifice.'

'What about grub then? Do we get everything with a can opener? I can't even boil an egg.'

'Don't worry. I'll take care of the grub. When you've learnt the art of survival cut off out in the bush, hungry enough to cut yourself a slice off a dead nigger's arse, roasting a chicken or frying a steak on an old-fashioned range is no problem.'

'If you say so,' said Munton, looking at the Rhodesian with renewed fear.

'Ever milked a cow?' said Haldane casually.

'Good God, no!'

'Not to worry. You can give me a hand in the morning. You'll soon get the feel of it. It's just like kneading a woman's tits.'

'Christ! You didn't spring me from stir just to be a bloody cowman?'

'No, but I've got to make a pretence of farming here. I took the place over as a going concern with the existing stock, eight cows, fifteen pigs and fifty battery hens. If I get rid of 'em all at once and show I'm not really a farmer, the estate manager is going to start wondering what the hell I am doing here. Idle curiosity, rumour and speculation and snooping peasants are the last things we need for our operation here. So I'm going through the motions of being a conventional farmer, and you're my right-hand man.'

'You mean when I'm not churning out the Lsd microdots, dyeing my hair and trimming my beard I'm to double up as a farm labourer. There are only twenty-four hours in the day, or hadn't you noticed?'

'I know,' replied Haldane with a mirthless grin. 'But they won't drag here like they would in the Scrubs, and you'd better remember it.'

'You know what,' said Munton. 'As I'm roughing it here and showing so much versatility and co-operation with management, I reckon we ought to re-negotiate that salary scale we talked about.'

'Bloody typical!' sneered Haldane, looking at him as if he was a turd. 'All you sods in this crapped-out country ever think about is trying to screw more money out of your employer, even when he's going broke. Then you think you can get him nationalised.'

'But look, guv, you're not broke, and a flat rate of five hundred quid a week is peanuts compared with what you'll be making on the six-hundred thousand microdots I'll be turning out with a six-day week. What about a small commission on top of the flat rate, say a quid on every thousand microdots? It'll give me more incentive to fill my quota, and I'll work flat out for you all the time, even when you're not watching.'

Haldane considered the pallid, under-sized figure of the Gingerman thoughtfully, and realised it was not a bad idea to have the little rat motivated by greed as well as fear.

'All right. That's OK by me,' he said at length. 'But tell me, what are you going to do with all this money you'll be earning? Are you reckoning on going into town and making a big splash with booze and tarts, till people start noticing you and wondering where you get your money from?'

'Leave it out, guv,' protested Munton indignantly. D'you think I'm some kind of a moron? Since you ask, I'm planning to save that money to set me up in the future, when I'm long gone from here and you're probably in stir. I'll open up a few separate Building Society accounts under different names, and pay in most of the money every month. I can buy National Savings Certificates as well, and National Investment Bonds. You bet your life I'll be putting this break to good use. Thank you for springing me, Your Honour!'

6

By January the microdot operation was in full production, working like a precision machine. In the prefabricated concrete building, warmed by an industrial space heater, Terry Munton in his clean white coat worked with an almost obsessional dedication for ten and sometimes twelve hours at a stretch. He was happy in his well-paid work, churning out the evil white tablets which went on the market at ten pence each in the coffee bars and discos, to bolster the inadequate personalities of escapists and losers.

Twice a week the Selous Scout took the production away in polythene bags and drove down to London on the M1, reaching his destination in under two hours. Having arranged by telephone a prior meeting place with Bradley Chawton, he delivered the microdots to the American, who organised the marketing and distribution of the hallucinogenics through connections opened up to him by his compatriot, Max Tordoff. The microdots were being sold as fast as Haldane could deliver them, and with typical entrepreneurial greed Chawton was always urging the Rhodesian to pull his finger out and step up production so that they could get even richer.

'Listen,' said Haldane angrily. 'Munton's doing bloody well up there with the equipment we've provided, and he's behaving himself so that there's no problem with security. Increasing production beyond six-hundred thousand a week is not possible without extra working space, extra equipment, and more manpower. You know the risks attached to building another shed and bringing in some other little crook who'll probably team up with Munton to screw us. Personally I'm all for getting rich in safety, even though it takes a bit longer. Big is not always beautiful, but I know that's heresy to you Yanks.'

'OK, OK,' said Chawton, rolling his fat cigar round his thin lips. 'You just keep that smooth little small-time number ticking over up there. I'll see about setting up another mine?'

* * *

It soon reached the attention of Scotland Yard's Drugs Squad that a powerful new source of Lsd microdots was supplying an ever-expanding market on the streets. The habitual pushers were loaded with microdots and peddled them vigorously in all the haunts of youth. But when they were pulled in and interrogated they knew nothing about their supplier. He was Mr Average, soberly dressed, with no distinguishing features. They couldn't pick him out from a line-up of bank managers, civil servants, or top ranking policemen. He made delivery from the boot of a car in a pub car park or other public place. Sometimes he made contact in the street and set up a meeting on a park bench or in a public lavatory. No transaction was ever completed until he'd driven his customer fast round a maze of London streets to make sure he hadn't got a tail.

Criminal Intelligence in liaison with the Drugs Squad soom realised that the expensively-arranged escape of Terence Munton from Wormwood Scrubs had everything to do with the sudden upsurge in the Lsd supply. Munton was a key figure in the illicit pharmaceutical business, and could only have been sprung for that reason. They concluded he must be set up in some cosy little laboratory somewhere with plenty of criminal money behind him, and until he could be found the pernicious, destructive hallucinogenic would continue its ravages on the lives of students, the youthful unemployed, the inadequate and the simple.

The failure to find the American criminal Bradley Chawton, now almost certainly in England, was another worrying factor for Detective Inspector Prosser. His factual mind hadn't yet leapt to the possible connection between Chawton and Munton in the boosted lsd supply, but he knew the American must have gone to ground in London and, being a proven entrepreneur, was already active in some lucrative criminal operation.

One day however Detective Sergeant Collins came into Prosser's office in a state of suppressed excitement.

'I think I've got a lead, guv'nor,' he exclaimed. 'Matthews of the Drugs Squad just told me they've been after a man called Max Tordoff for years. They reckon he's a cocaine importer and dealer, and supplies all the Mayfair playboys and the *creme de la creme* with their Fairy Snow. But he's too bloody clever to be caught, never leaves a single opening or a loose end.'

'Is he in our files?' said DI Prosser.

'I wouldn't have thought so. He's got no form. He's a Yank and has been settled here since the end of World War Two. He runs a thriving antique and fine arts business in Bond Street and has a house in Wembley. But what's of interest to us is that there's another Yank moved in with him since last September, somebody by the name of Paul Rossiter who has a Resident's Permit from the Home Office, subject to re-assessment after nine months. He's apparently in London researching a book on the effects of the Milton Schulman monetary theories put into sustained operation on the British economy. As any associate of Tordoff is of interest to the Drugs Squad they photographed this Rossiter from a parked car as he left the house in Wembley. Matthews gave me this photo print of him that I reckon looks very promising. What do you think, guv?'

He passed over the full-face photograph to Prosser who studied it carefully. It showed a square face with heavy black-rimmed spectacles, neatly trimmed moustache and small pointed Imperial beard. The black hair had been allowed to grow long so that it half-covered his ears and was brushed straight back with a central parting, giving him a half-raffish, half-intellectual look. At first glance it was the face of a professional man with a certain foppish pretentiousness. The style of the beard was a century out of date and did not suit the shape of the face.

As he studied it more closely Prosser became convinced that the several excrescences had been added merely to blur the main contours of the face and prevent recognition. He placed alongside it the FBI photograph of Bradley Chawton, comparing the thin mouth, the narrow close-set eyes, the shape of the jaw and the forehead, topped by its head of hair in one picture and its prison crew cut in the other. The bespectacled and bearded face was fuller in the cheeks than the lean wolfish face of the convict. But that could be attributable to the months of soft, rich living he would have indulged in after all the rigours and deprivations of Federal custody.

'I see what you mean,' said Prosser slowly. 'Paul Rossiter could be Bradley Chawton being harboured by his fellow countryman, Tordoff.'

'So do we pull him in then and check his dabs?' said DS Collins eagerly.

The inspector considered it carefully, realising how such a positive move could backfire on him. He knew all too well what happened to over-zealous detectives who stuck their necks out by harassing ethnic minorities or foreign nationals on insufficient evidence. It was open season on coppers in all the political coverts, and if he made an embarrassing blunder with Paul Rossiter every senior officer at the Yard right up to the Commissioner would piously turn round and shit on him. If he survived on the Force at all it would be as a wolly on traffic duty in the Mall.

'We're not a hundred per cent sure it's Chawton, are we?' he said. 'It could be a coincidental resemblance, and how could this Rossiter have got a Resident's Permit from the Home Office unless he had proper credentials as a US citizen? If he should be a bona fide American academic we'd get a hell of a lot of flak via the Home Office from the U.S. Embassy.'

'His dabs would clinch it,' said Collins. 'Why don't I go round to his pad in Wembley posing as a market researcher for Breakfast TV, give him a questionnaire to fill in and lend him my ballpoint? We'd get a viable finger and thumb print off that.'

'No, I don't think that's a good idea,' said Prosser. 'If Rossiter really is Chawton he's sharp enough to suss you like a shot and know we're on to him. He'd just go underground, change his name and face and address, and it could be months before we got another smell of him. Then we won't know what racket he's beavering away at. I think we'll go softly softly with Mr Paul Rossiter. Let him go on with his researches and put him in the Target Criminal frame.'

'Do you think we can get permission to put a wire-trap on his phone, guv?'

'No, I don't have much hope of that with a U.S. national. One thing you can do though is make some discreet enquiries at the U.S. Embassy about Mr Paul Rossiter. They'll know his background and origins, his Alma Mater and his blood group and where he spent his Sophomore Year.'

'Will do, guv.'

'It won't hurt to let it go for a few more weeks. The Yanks will have to wait a bit longer for Chawton. I've already been told by an irate FBI man on the transatlantic phone that we couldn't find an elephant in a phone booth.'

7

As the winter progressed the police who were trying desperately to locate the source of the new LSD supply suddenly had an unexpected piece of luck which pointed them towards Northamptonshire. One night in February when the weather turned bad and the first real snow of the winter came, there was a break-in at the pharmaceutical laboratories of Thomas Kerridge Ltd, in Welwyn Garden City. Apart from a large number of barbiturates several kilos of hydrazeme hydrate, an ingredient of LSD, had been stolen.

On the same night fifty miles further north on the road to Kettering a large Volvo estate car skidded in the snow and slithered nose-first into a ditch. When the police found it abandoned there the snow all round it was trampled hard by numerous feet as if several men had tried urgently to manhandle it back on to the road.

A cursory inspection of the vehicle revealed that some white powder had been spilled on the carpet of the boot close to the tail-gate as if a bag had burst on removal. As a routine process a sample of this powder was sent to the police laboratory for analysis, and was promptly identified as hydrazeme hydrate. Thus the Regional Crime Squad officers working on the drugs theft at Welwyn Garden City came to know they'd found the vehicle which had been used in the raid, and also that it had been delivering the stolen material to some destination in Northamptonshire.

A check on the ownership of the Volvo showed it to belong to a Charles Claude Leplar who lived at Harrow-on-the-Hill and had reported his car as stolen on the morning of its discovery in the ditch near Kettering.

Leplar was middle-aged, bald, florid and evidently prosperous, living in a large detached house in a tree-lined suburban road. He claimed to be a consultant heating engineer who dealt mainly in solar panel heating installations and traded by advertising from his private address.

His high state of nervous apprehension when detectives came to question him about his car gave rise to instant suspicion. But the detectives played it coolly and didn't press him too hard, even though they were highly dubious about the time lag between the actual disappearance of Leplar's car and his reporting of the theft. They pretended to be satisfied and went away, but they immediately began intensive enquiries into the whole background, life-style and social connections of Charles Claude Leplar.

Although he had no police record and no known connections with the underworld, there had been complaints against him from members of the public about an electronic control box for the ordinary domestic heating system which Leplar had been marketing to the credulous and unwary. He claimed it would reduce fuel consumption by thirty per cent without any diminution of heat output, and was an absolute bargain at eight-hundred pounds. The furious customers who'd paid good money for a cheap and worthless gadget wanted Leplar prosecuted for fraudulent misrepresentation. But having looked carefully into his activities and the latitude allowed by the law, the North London police could see there was insufficient evidence against Leplar to secure a conviction. No charges were brought, but Leplar was given a stern warning which he was duly mindful of when drawing up the sales prospectus of his next ingenious gadget for saving the householder money.

On discovering that Leplar was a thriving con man, the Regional Crime Squad detectives working on the drugs theft case were now strongly suspicious that Leplar had played a conspicuous part in the Welwyn Garden City pharmaceutical robbery. But a bit of powder in the back of his car which could have been spilt there by other thieves was all they had against him. So rather than warn Leplar that they were on to him and thus cause him to give his criminal associates a wide berth for a long time, they decided to keep him under unobtrusive surveillance for weeks and months if necessary, building up a profile of his way of life and a dossier on all the people with whom he came into contact.

It was through this endeavour that DI Prosser of Criminal Intelligence at Scotland Yard received an enquiry from the Regional Crime Squad about the bona fides of a Mr Paul Rossiter who lived at Wembley. Did C11 have any information of a suspicious nature about Rossiter's activities or possible criminal connections in London? The reason for the enquiry was that he'd recently been observed in a West End wine bar in the company of a Charles Claude leplar who was under surveillance as prime suspect in a recent robbery at a pharmaceutical laboratory.

The implications of Rossiter's connection with such a man banished all Prosser's former reservations about going soft on a suspect because he was an American national.

'So the facial resemblance we noticed of Rossiter to Chawton was no coincidence after all,' said Prosser. 'If Chawton is involved with thieves at a pharmaceutical factory he must be well into the drugs racket, which was one of his specialities in the States. The stuff that this Leplar is suspected of stealing is used in the manufacture of LSD, and we know from the Drugs Squad that there's no let-up in the supply of microdots. In fact they're getting even more plentiful on the streets, and knocking off the occasional pusher is only tinkering with the problem. The number of deaths and serious injuries among the young idiots taking trips on microdots is reaching epidemic proportions. We've got them trying to leap-frog over oncoming double-deckers, flying out of tower block windows and off bridges like Batman and Robin, trying to break through walls with their heads. In fact LSD will soon be a more serious blood-letter among the young than Japanese motor bikes if we don't dry up the source. We'll pull in this Rossiter now and confront him with the identity of Bradley Chawton. His finger prints will settle it one way or the other.

And if he should be an innocent, law-abiding Yank after all this, I'll face up to the firing squad.'

DI Prosser ordered his car and accompanied by DS Collins drove round to Tordoff's house in Wembley, where Rossiter was known to be staying. But the house was closed up and they couldn't raise anybody. They didn't have a warrant to break in and search it, so the only alternative was to visit Max Tordoff at his high class antiques and fine arts boutique in Bond Street.

Tordoff was in his fifties, an amiable, silver-haired, stoop-shouldered man with rimless bifocals and naive blue eyes. He looked more like a professor strayed away from some university campus than a wheeler-dealer or a crook.

'Paul Rossiter?' he said. 'Yes, I stood sponsor for him when he needed a work permit. He has been staying in my house for several weeks, but he moved out about a fortnight ago. He said he'd done all the research on his book that he could achieve in London, so he was moving on.'

'Did he say where to?'

'No, he said his plans were flexible. He may have gone to consult some leading economists at Oxford, or he may have travelled up to Edinburgh to visit with an old professor whose pupil he used to be. He may even have gone back to the States by now.'

'Didn't he leave a forwarding address?' said Prosser, striving hard to master his irritation with this bland, plausible crook.

'He did not, because he didn't really know where he'd settle. But I expect I shall be hearing from him eventually. Is there any message you'd like me to hand on?'

'No,' said Prosser shortly. 'It's just a routine enquiry about his Resident's Permit. I daresay it'll keep.'

'Ok. Fine. I'll tell him to contact you just as soon as he surfaces.'

'You do that,' said Prosser. 'We'll look forward to hearing from him.'

But as the two detectives walked back to their car Prosser was less than pleased.

'Rossiter's been tipped off and gone

underground,' he said angrily. 'And I'll swear that bloody Tordoff knows all about it. He was laughing at us.'

'Maybe Chawton spotted that Leplar had a tail on him when they last met, or possibly he had a contact in the U.S. Embassy who tipped him off that we were making discreet enquiries. We should have taken a chance on it and pulled him in weeks ago. We're not going to find him now in a hurry.'

Prosser gave him an aggrieved look and said nothing.

'And speaking of his contacts,' went on Collins, 'Chawton must have got some real high-powered help from somewhere. How else did he wangle a nine-months residential permit from the Home Office? He's only a lousy criminal on the run with a fake passport. How did he suddenly become respectable enough to be vetted and given clearance and privileged status by the Home Office Department for Immigration and aliens?'

'I know. That's been bothering me as well,' said the inspector. 'In fact it was what put us completely off the scent when we first considered the facial resemblance between Rossiter and Chawton.'

'It stinks a bit, doesn't it guv?'

'Obviously there's a mole in that damned rabbit warren at Queen Anne's Gate who really knows his way about, and Chawton's associates have got to him. Maybe when we do nail Chawton and the whole conspiracy is revealed, we'll also get to know who they've bought in the Home Office.'

Shortly afterwards however, Bradley Chawton and his presumed connection with the LSD microdot laboratory became a rather lower priority for C11, and was removed to the back burner. Over Easter there came the famous conquest of 'Fort Knox' in Shoreditch, the highly organised take-over of Security Express Headquarters, with the removal of five tons of untraceable paper currency and not a clue left behind as to the identity of the perpetrators. All the efforts and resources of Criminal Intelligence were desperately mobilised in a supreme effort to find some lead however slight. It was the face-saving operation of all time.

8

As the winter drew to its bitter, protracted close in Northamptonshire Terry Munton felt that he was part of the scenery. The only thing that worried him was his ever-present fear of the grim and ferocious-looking Henry Haldane, who at first had guarded him like a kind of criminal imbecile always liable to fall into the hands of the police.

When Munton had grown his hair long and cultivated a bushy beard which, like his hair he dyed black once a week, Haldane took him fairly often into the bigger towns like Peterborough and Northampton for a night's entertainment in the pubs and clubs. He realised that Munton, a gregarious Londoner, wouldn't be a contented worker for long if he was totally imprisoned on the lonely farm without the sights and sounds and smells of city life. So Haldane judged it was safe to loose him up in the larger

East Anglian towns where the chances of his meeting an old London acquaintance were negligible.

However, Haldane drew the line at letting Munton use his car, a large Datsun estate which was owned legally and registered in Haldane's name, for Munton did not hold his liquor very well. The last thing Haldane wanted was the police making routine enquiries at Woodfield Hollow Farm over a drunk-driving offence.

Occasionally Munton was allowed to stay the night in town in order to go home with some whore to get laid. Before he went Haldane always read him the riot act, describing in bloodcurdling terms what would happen to him if he shot his mouth off in pillow talk about who he was, where he lived and what he was doing at the farm.

'I'll pick you up at nine o'clock in the morning at the junction of Westgate and Broad Street,' said Haldane. 'And don't be bloody late. And don't start running away if you see a copper.'

'Leave it out, guv'nor,' said Munton

in an aggrieved tone. 'You don't have to chaperone me around like a nanny. I've been doing my own thing for a good many years now.'

'Sure,' sneered Haldane, 'in and out of stir, you dumb arsehole.'

'Why can't I buy my own car and live my own social life?' grumbled Munton.

'I've told you, I don't want any vehicle traceable to you at Woodfield Hollow. As soon as people know you're living there they'll start wondering why you're there and who you really are. I'd prefer you to stay under cover all the time for complete security, but I know that's not feasible. So I'm giving you a social life provided you don't do anything stupid to attract attention. I've got to trust you while I go down to London, and so far it's been all right. Business is booming and everybody's happy. You're a valued member of society with a worthwhile job, so let's keep it that way. Don't rock the boat, Munton, or I'll have your guts. The fuzz can have what's left.'

So Munton tried as hard as was in his nature to keep this wholesome threat in mind. As he wasn't allowed a car or any other traceable form of transport, he bought himself a bicycle from a second-hand cycle shop in Corby, and used it for short excursions to the local pubs and villages and the nearby town.

★ ★ ★

One blustering night in March when the wind howled round the eaves and gables of Woodfield Hollow, Terry Munton was relaxing in the sitting-room before a roaring log fire, contentedly despatching one can of ale after another as he watched the large screen of the colour television. He was enjoying a programme called 'Our Prisons' and giving off self-congratulatory chuckles over his own contrasted life-style as he looked in from the outside on the familiar squalid interiors of famous penitentiaries, and listened knowingly to all the do-gooders pontificating about his rehabilitation and what was best for him and his kind in the pure administration of penal absolution.

Henry Haldane was doing his usual

late-night patrol of the outlying farm buildings, accompanied by Angus the Doberman, to make sure that no unauthorised snoopers or vagrants were anywhere near the precious laboratory.

Suddenly the Rhodesian froze in instant awareness of danger as the headlights of an approaching car flared up in the deserted lane, unmistakably heading for the farm in the hollow. The hound tensed beside Haldane and a menacing rumble sounded in its throat. It seemed to know, as Haldane knew, that anybody coming to the farm at that hour could mean nothing but trouble. Haldane gripped the dog hard by its choker chain as the car, recklessly driven, swerved erratically into the farmyard and stopped with all its lights full on.

A man got out, shielding his eyes defensively against the bright glare of the torch which Haldane shone in his face. It was Bradley Chawton still wearing spectacles and beard, dressed in dark felt hat and belted raincoat like a thirties gangster, and looking equally harassed and desperate.

'Christ! What the hell are you doing here?' exclaimed Haldane tensely. 'Are you hot?'

'Just a bit warm, is all,' said Chawton, trying to sound casual. 'Max Tordoff's got a stoolpigeon inside Scotland Yard. He tipped me off that Charlie Leplar's been under surveillance for weeks, and I had a meet with the dumb cocksucker only two days ago. The fuzz are bound to be on to me. Anyway I'm sure as hell not waiting about to be interviewed.'

'But coming straight here to the factory, you'll turn us all in!' exclaimed Haldane with growing anger.

'Relax, you asshole! I know what I'm doing. I won't stay long in this hole, you can be sure of that. Just a night or two till I get fixed up.'

'What about the car?' persisted Haldane. 'Is that traceable to you?'

'Of course not. I lifted it in Piccadily from alongside a parking meter. It's clean. I shall need it when I move on. I could use a drink right now and some grub. So what about showing me some of that famous British hospitality instead of keeping me out here rapping all night?'

Still fuming with anger and a growing unease that things had started to fall apart in a hitherto flawless operation, Haldane showed his unwelcome guest into the farm kitchen, set a bottle of whisky and a glass in front of him, and told him to get what food he wanted from the freezer.

'What about marketing and distributing the microdots?' said Haldane. 'If you're not going to be on the job in London any more, how can I deliver in bulk?'

'You'll have to fix up your own meets with the middle men,' replied Chawton. 'I've got a list of 'em here, their phone numbers and addresses and the best times to make contact. It won't cause you much extra work, and there's no risk.'

'So you're going into retirement and still drawing your piece of the action while I do your share of the work as well as my own?' pursued Haldane with increasing resentment. 'What's Don Carrington got to say about your own personal UDI?'

'Don doesn't know about it yet. I

couldn't raise him on the telephone, and I wasn't risking a visit to his house just in case the lousy fuzz have got a line on him as well. But Don will go along with anything I have to do. No sweat. I don't aim to go in retirement either. That's not my scene. I figured I can set up another laboratory round here and beef up production to double what you're managing here.'

'Oh, the Big Ideas man again, eh?' sneered Haldane. 'Anything I can do, you can make it twice as big.'

'Sure,' countered Chawton with equal rancour. 'You're only a dumb amateur who can work under supervision when somebody's drawn you a picture. Do you seriously reckon you'd ever have got this show on the road without me and Don?'

'So tell me then,' persisted Haldane furiously. 'Are you planning to move the contractors in here and set up another prefabricated building with a whole new range of chemical equipment? And have you got another first-rate production chemist lined up that you're going to spring from stir? You said you were only staying here a night or two, so what do you have in mind? The instant tenancy of another of Golden Boy's farms?'

'Better than that,' replied Chawton with an evil grin. 'Our worthy patron, Golden Boy, is going to help me out again, though he doesn't know it yet. I'm going to stay as a privileged guest at Aldingbourne Manor while I look around the district for factory floor space.'

Haldane stared at him aghast, almost unable to believe what he'd heard.

'Stay at the Manor? Do you mean you're just going to walk into Carvell's country home up here and tell his wife she's got to take you in as one of the family, or else?'

'Sure,' said Chawton calmly. 'Can you think of a better idea? Golden Boy is into us so far already that he's practically one of the share-holders. Giving me five-star accommodation at the stately home is nothing to what he's done for us already. His little wife is going to be eternally grateful to me for giving her the option when I could just as easily blow the whistle and land her old man in stir.'

'Christ! You're dumb!' swore Haldane furiously. 'You'll blow the whole operation and bring the fuzz down on us in droves. They'll be swarming all over this farm like bluebottles round a corpse. Don't you realise the Manor will be crawling with tittle-tattling domestic servants? As soon as you foist yourself on the house they'll start wondering what a thug like you is doing with Mrs Carvell. They'll whisper and spread the gossip. Scandal up at the Manor. In any case Mrs Carvell might not be so easy to intimidate as her husband with his guilty conscience. I'm told the Lady Lucinda is the daughter of a Duke, so why should she stand for anything from a bloody roughneck like you? She's only got to call the police and hand you over for threatening behaviour. Then it'll all come out. We've got a hell of a good thing going here, our own private mint churning out money unlimited, and there's no way they can ever get on to us while it's like it is. But you come crashing in here and you're going to put it all at risk by being the big macho he-man with the Lady of the Manor! For God's sake, why not just stay here with me and Munton if you're hot? What are you trying to prove?'

Bradley Chawton laughed in his face contemptuously.

'So it's all true about your monarchy-loving snots!' he jeered. 'You're still a lot of grovelling, knee-bending, cap-in-hand peasants before a better class of person. This is the twentieth century, for God's sake! And you're still cowering in superstitious dread before somebody with a bit of social rank who might have rubbed shoulders with a dook and lives up at the Manor. Wise up, feller. Don't get fazed by the oldie-worldie limey bullshit about class. You're a new world man, aren't you, even if the niggers have kicked your ass out of there? A man is a man who has to shit once a day, nothing else. And he's got a price tag on him. It doesn't matter what bloody feudal wrappings he puts round himself to bullshit the ignorant.'

But for Henry Haldane the situation had reached a far more desperate stage than any intellectual argument. Words couldn't rationalise anything in this crisis. He could see like a clairvoyant the whole course of the impending disaster if this brash, cocky, arrogant Yank was left free to operate at his own reckless mental level. With his cover blown and the police after him he was a source of great danger whatever he did.

Swept along by the surge of irresistible violence that suddenly possessed him, Haldane suddenly grabbed the full bottle of whisky and swung it round in a ferocious arc at Chawton's head. It struck the side of his head between his left ear and temple, hurling him across the kitchen floor, showering everything with whisky and shards of glass. Chawton skidded along the floor and landed with a crash against the old wooden cupboard. He lay there still, sprawled in a grotesque posture with one side of his head a crushed mass of blood, splintered bone and brain tissue, and a fixed, glassy look in his eye. Haldane was conversant enough with death to see at a glance that Chawton would trouble him no more with his grandiose, big-time, criminal adventurism.

Terry Munton in the sitting room heard the violent crash above the civilised murmur of his television, and ran immediately into the kitchen to see what had happened.

Haldane was still standing near the table with the neck of the shattered bottle clenched in his hand and a look of such diabolical savagery on his face that Terry cringed before him defensively, wondering if he was going to be next.

'Jesus Christ, guv,' he muttered, swiftly assessing the damage to the victim. 'You sure as hell did a number on him! What did he do? Who is the geezer anyway?'

'A bloody menace who was going to blow the whistle on us,' snarled Haldane. 'I did you a favour. He was after you, the Gingerman. He'd got a line on you somehow and was asking for you here.'

'God! No!'

'I told him you weren't here, but he wouldn't have it and wouldn't go away, so I had to croak him.'

'But how the hell could he know I'm

here? I've never seen him in my life. Is he law?'

'No, but he knew all about you. You've not been shooting your bloody mouth off to some broad in a pub, have you?'

'No, no! I swear it!' protested Terry desperately. 'But if this bugger's sussed me there could be others. Maybe it's time I flew the coop, guv.'

'No, not necessarily,' said Haldane. 'No need to panic yet. I found out from what he said he's on his own. Nobody else knows he was coming here after you. He was working on a hunch. That's why I knew it was safe to top him. If we can tuck him up out of sight and remove all traces, that'll be the end of it. You'll be safe.'

'Jesus, guv, I hope you're right,' muttered Terry, glancing at the stiffening corpse with mounting dread, already half-convinced that he was responsible for the death.

'It's for your benefit I had to get rid of him, so you're in on it,' went on Haldane menacingly as if he read Terry's thoughts. 'You'd better give me a hand to get him out of sight.'

'Sure, guv. Anything you say,' gulped Terry. 'Where d'you want him planted?'

'Go and get the wheelbarrow and a shovel for the burial detail. We'll think of some place.'

While Terry was gone Haldane methodically emptied the dead man's pockets and transferred everything to his own person. A minute later Terry returned, and together they hoisted the sagging corpse of Bradley Chawton into the old farm wheelbarrow. They set off into the darkness, leaving the farmhouse under the sole protection of Angus the Doberman. With Haldane leading the way with an electric torch and carrying a spade over his shoulder, Terry wheeled the heavy barrow across the farmyard, through the orchard gate and out into the pasture land beyond. It was heavy going for the earth was soft with the recent rain, and Chawton seemed to get heavier with every yard. Terry puffed and sweated along like a Chinese coolie under his rickshaw, while Haldane strode on ahead with a lordly air, showing the way with his torch beam.

About a mile from the farm he opened the gate into a wood and led the way over a grassy ride to a clearing about fifty yards square. Swiftly Haldane marked out the grave in the turf, six feet by two feet. Carefully he skimmed the turf off, cutting it into squares and stacking it neatly for future use. Then he handed the spade to Munton, his beast of burden.

'OK, get cracking,' he said curtly. 'I want it at least five feet deep, and we haven't got all bloody night.'

The sodden earth was heavy and viscous, clinging stubbornly to the spade as Terry toiled and grafted harder than he'd ever worked in his life. The sweat poured off him, but every time he stopped for a breather the watching supervisor prodded him remorselessly to new efforts.

'Come on, work, you idle little shit!' he snarled. 'Even the bloody kaffirs dig better graves than you can. If it wasn't for your messy existence the bugger would be still alive. I had to do him in to save you going back to stir, and don't forget it.'

'OK, guv. I appreciate it. I really do,' panted Terry, desperately summoning up new reserves to sustain his aching muscles.

When Haldane grudgingly admitted that the grave was deep enough they tumbled Chawton into it, piled the earth on top of him and stamped it down thoroughly. When it was hard and packed to the level of the original soil under the turf, Haldane, a proven expert in the technique of the unmarked grave, skillfully replaced the squares of turf that had been stripped off, so that there was no sign of any disturbance in the grassy terrain. Then he ordered Munton to load the remaining soil into the wheelbarrow and take it away to scatter it in all directions among the trees. Finally Haldane planted some brambles on the grave and declared himself satisfied.

When they arrived back at the farm it only remained to clean up the mess in the kitchen and dispose of Chawton's stolen car, a chore which Haldane felt safe enough in delegating to Terry.

'You can drive a motor, can't you?' he said.

'Sure, guv. I can hot-wire it if I have to.'

'No need for that. The key's still in it. Sling your bike in the back and drive it to one of the public car parks in Kettering. Then you can cycle back here before morning. Put some gloves on before you go near it. If the fuzz should ever test it for dabs we don't want them finding out that the Gingerman is living and thriving in the Kettering area, burying people.'

9

For some weeks after the burial of the mysterious night visitor Terry lived and worked in a state of high nervous tension, wondering if the dead man who'd known about him had left any other trails to the farm. But gradually as no other menacing spectre from the past turned up to trouble him, and as Haldane seemed to have dismissed the gruesome visitation as if it had never happened, Terry concluded that any threat the man brought had indeed died with him.

Terry felt a return to his old cheerful optimism, working hard every day in his laboratory and gratefully enjoying the leisure hours of his much appreciated freedom. One thing which that night of violence had instilled in him was an even deeper fear and respect for his grim employer. The murderous ferocity with which the intruder had been killed, and the ruthless efficiency with which he'd been disposed of afterwards left Terry in no doubt that a similar fate awaited him if he ever crossed Haldane or became a source of danger to him.

Soon it was springtime with the countryside growing green again and the days getting longer and warmer. Even though there was no poetry in him Munton started to feel more alive with a greater sense of well-being after the long grey oppressive winter months in the desolate outback. He explored the countryside a great deal on his bike, visiting all the pubs and striking up acquaintanceships with the countryfolk. Terry was a cheerful extravert, ready to buy anybody a drink and chat them up about life in general, so that even the wary and closed-in villagers began to react towards the little Londoner with a partial thaw. It was good to be among people again as an equal free citizen, not an inferior being in a cage. Nobody stared at him in a disparaging or accusing way. His picture hadn't been in the papers since his escape last October, and then it hadn't been camouflaged by its present black-dyed, bird's nest beard. The fuzz were still looking for the Gingerman with ginger hair and moustache.

There were moments when he genuinely forgot he was an escaped convict on the run, and his life seemed full of promise as he tucked away his weekly pay in his several Building Society accounts. But sometimes in the small hours he started awake after a terrible nightmare in which he was back in Wormwood Scrubs, being threatened by one of the hard men. He was bathed in sweat, and it was as if a black weight of depression was crushing all the joy out of him. But Terry was resilient and he soon bounced back. Inevitably he found himself a woman.

She was a woman farmer who owned and worked her own small property, Vicar's Hill Farm, which was about seven miles from Woodfield Hollow on the way to Grafton Underwood. Her name was Shelagh Fossett. The locals called her Sugar Fossett, for in her youth she'd been the beauty of the countryside whom every man had tried to possess. She'd had so many men all through her youth that it had slipped her mind to grab one of them in passing, and at the age of thirty-five she was still unmarried. Both her parents were recently dead and she lived alone, farming her hundred acres like any man, doing most of the work herself with the aid of seasonal labour.

Sugar Fossett was a well-built woman with an open cheerful face, still remarkably handsome even though her early prettiness had faded into the ruddy tan of a countrywoman who spent most of her life out of doors. She dressed in riding breeches and boots and a man's open-necked shirt, with an army surplus combat jacket when the weather turned cold. Nobody had seen her in a woman's dress since her early twenties when she used to get squired around to Hunt Balls and other rural functions.

It was on a fine April evening that Munton, cycling down the 'B' road past Vicar's Hill Farm saw Sugar Fossett driving her dozen cows out of the milking shed back to the adjoining pasture. He got off his bike to admire the view, for she was a fine figure of a woman with

117

her short blonde hair, her rosy cheeks and large dimensions. She was taller than Terry and bigger all round, but that didn't deter him. He'd always liked a real armful, something he could get his teeth into.

'Hullo darling,' said Munton with his usual city slicker's approach and the frankness of lust in his eyes. 'Are there any more at home like you?'

'Why?' she said, with a swift disparaging glance at Munton's slightly built, stoop-shouldered figure and sallow skin. 'You look as if one would be too many for your state of health.'

'Oh, very quick!' applauded Terry, by no means discouraged. 'Are you the farmer's wife then?'

'No, I'm the farmer.'

'Oh?' said Terry in surprise. 'You own this place, and run it too?'

'That's right.'

'You live alone?'

'Fortunately, yes.'

'Don't you need a man about the place?'

'When I need labour I hire it at the

going rate,' she said crisply. 'But I'm always better off doing the job myself, which is why I don't have the time to hang about gossiping.'

With that she turned her back on him and went back into the milking shed, where she could be heard crashing about with buckets and other utensils. Munton pedalled off thoughtfully on his bike, but he came back the next evening when it was dark, and watched from behind a hedge as the lights went on in the stone farmhouse at the end of Sugar Fossett's day. He watched her making her last rounds for the night, closing down the hen coops, having a last look in the byre where she'd got a cow ready to go into labour. He thought sentimentally it was the kind of peaceful, trouble-free, undemanding life that would have been just right for him rather than the dangerous, squalid rough-house of the East End slums. If only he'd been born with roots and a woman like that to work for and care for, he would certainly never have fallen foul of the law and wasted so many of his best years in stir.

Outside in the dark he watched through the uncurtained window as she had her evening meal in the big farmhouse kitchen. She cut herself thick slices from a boiled ham and fetched beer in a jug from a stone pantry adjoining the kitchen. Afterwards she switched on the television in her chintzy sitting room, but soon dozed off in the chair before it. At ten o'clock she went upstairs to bed, and as she didn't draw the curtains in her bedroom either Munton got a good eyeful of Sugar Fossett in the raw.

She unbuttoned her shirt to reveal her large pendulous breasts. Munton stood rooted to the spot, his eyes starting out of his head, as she peeled off the rest of her clothes. Then she had a quick sponge down at a wash-hand stand and dusted herself liberally with talcum powder before leaping into bed and switching the light out. Only then did Munton make his disconsolate and frustrated way back to the morose or bit of Henry Haldane.

He found himself returning to Vicar's

Hill Farm night after night to be present at Sugar Fossett's bedding down. He had a burning compulsion to be near her, to observe her farming and domestic routine, and to tease himself with prurient imaginings.

One night as he watched her going round the hen coops he stepped too far out from cover in his excitement, and although it was dark the beam of her torch embraced his movement for a second. She caught it from the corner of her eye, and turned the full beam on the lurking figure as he skulked behind a pig-sty wall. She stood still for a moment staring at him without any sign of fear, for she vaguely remembered him as the oddball who'd come past on his bike a week or two ago and tried to chat her up.

'What do you want?' she said at length. 'Who are you?'

'My name's Terry,' he said. 'What's yours?'

'Why are you hanging about here at this time of night?'

'I don't know. I just like being here. I

like watching you, the way you do things, the way you live here on your own. I'm not going to pinch anything. I often come here and watch you turn in for the night, standing at your window and that.'

'Oh,' she said, slightly amused, 'I suppose I ought to draw my curtains before I strip off. It never occurred to me I could get an audience out here. I never had one before in thirty years. You're some kind of a peeping tom, are you?'

'Not usually. It's just that you interest me. Well, I mean, a woman living out here in the backwoods alone, running a farm, not scared of anything.'

'I've got nothing against peeping toms,' she said with a chuckle. 'You must have a very frustrating life. I suppose I ought to feel flattered at my age. Now you're here you may as well come in for a drink.'

'Well, that's very civil of you. Don't mind if I do,' said Terry with a feeling of triumph.

In the big stone-paved farm kitchen with its modern Aga cooker and its old-fashioned pots and pans she fetched him a mug of her powerful home-brewed beer and a wedge of bread and cheese. Sugar Fossett watched him curiously, for all her following hitherto had been sturdy peasant stock of the Northamptonshire countryside. She'd never known a nimble-witted Londoner before, and this new admirer who hung about in the dark watching her bedroom window to see her strip off was like someone from an alien world.

'You weren't born and brought up round here, were you?' she enquired.

'Not me. London, the East End. Plaistow to be exact.'

'What do you do then? I mean work at, when you're not peeping through windows at ladies undressing.'

'I'm a research chemist,' he said proudly.

'What does that mean?'

'I work for a pharmaceutical company, trying to develop new life-saving drugs for killer diseases like cancer and arthritis. I had a big part in that new drug Opren that everybody thought was so marvellous. But when it turned out it was killing people as a side-effect, I got upset and had a nervous breakdown because I thought it was all my fault. The quack ordered me a complete rest and a change so I wouldn't go right round the twist. I came out here into the country.'

'Where are you staying?'

'Oh, it's on a farm a few miles from Kettering. A friend of mine runs it. He's offered to let me stay for a few weeks till I get my bottle back.'

'Which farm are you on?' she persisted. 'Do I know your friend?'

'No, shouldn't think so,' said Terry hastily. 'He's only been there since last September when it became vacant.'

'Oh, it's a tenant farm then? Not one of those on the Aldingbourne Manor Estate?'

'Yes, I suppose so. Woodfield Hollow it's called.'

'Oh yes. I heard that farm was changing hands. I used to know Fred Pyke and his family. He got very fed up with EEC rules and regulations, and said he was going to chance his arm in New Zealand. I hope he's not just got out of the frying pan.'

'He'll be back in a year or two,' said Terry. 'I'd put my shirt on it. A lazy bugger who can't cut it here certainly won't stand much chance overseas.'

As she started showing an unhealthy interest in the new tenant at Woodfield Hollow, Terry hurriedly changed the subject. He started telling her a creative fictional sob story about his own tragic personal life.

'I used to be married, but it didn't work out. She said I spent too many hours working and had no time to take her out. When things were going badly over the Opren business and I got depressed, she said she couldn't take it any more because I was making her depressed. So she went home to mum who encouraged her in it, and took our little girl Sandra with her. Sandra was a dear little thing, only three and a half at the time. Let's see, she'd be five now.'

'You mean you've not seen her since?' said Sugar Fossett compassionately.

Terry could see he'd got to her with the human sympathy angle. She'd be crying in her beer next and trying to mother him. He'd already decided he wanted to be mothered by Sugar Fossett.

'Never from that day to this. Helen said she wanted a divorce and a clean break, and in return she wasn't going to insist on any maintenance or a half-share in the home. I was too ill at the time to argue about anything, so I went along with it. Then she told me she'd got this other bloke hanging about who wanted to marry her, and she didn't want me hovering in the background trying to see Sandra and scaring her new boyfriend off. So I just bowed out like a perfect gent. It means for the rest of my life I'll be able to pass my own daughter in the street without ever recognising her.'

'But I think that's terrible,' said Sugar Fossett indignantly. 'How could a woman be so selfish and cruel?'

'It takes all sorts,' said Terry philosophically. 'It didn't do my depression any good at the time, but I reckon I'm getting over it. I don't look back. The future's all I've got.'

'And how long will you be staying at Woodfield Hollow?'

'Till my shrink gives me a clean bill of health, I suppose. Then it'll be back to the Smoke to an empty house, and clocking on again at that damned drugs factory.'

He glanced up at the old wooden-cased clock with its big brass pendulum ticking away robustly on the wall.

'Christ! Is it that time already? I'd better be off. Do you mind if I call again sometime? It's comforting to have a natter with a sympathetic listener.'

'Of course,' she said cordially. 'Come any time you like as long as I'm not out working. Don't waste any more time peeping through my windows, will you? You know the old saying: When you've seen one you've seen them all.'

10

Thenceforth Terry called on Sugar Fossett regularly in the evenings. He told Haldane he was going into Kettering or Corby on his bike for an evening in the pubs. The Selous Scout grumbled a bit, gave him a dire warning about shooting his mouth off, and let him go.

Sometimes Sugar cooked him a meal of plain farmhouse fare. At other times they watched TV companionably in the sitting-room, or they just sat round the large kitchen table talking for hours.

She just knew him as Terry (surname not mentioned) and he called her Sugar, which she told him was the pet name her father had given her when she was five years old. She didn't mention it was the appreciative name given her by every gratified young yokel who'd managed to tumble her in the hayfield or at harvest time when she was young and sweet.

Terry was very much a man of the world and an amusing talker. The little human anecdotes, ludicrous scrapes and bizarre situations which he'd witnessed or heard about in prison he retold to her with suitable embellishments, ascribing them to the eccentrics and oddballs who worked with him in the mythical pharmaceutical factory.

Sugar had a dry, astute sense of humour, and he enjoyed the sound of her hearty laughter. She could drink and hold her beer like any man, and he detected in her a robust integrity which appealed strongly to him, even though in his own life he'd always been a stranger to honesty. More than anything he felt he belonged here with this kind and courageous woman who treated him as an equal and a comrade. He felt at one with this slightly sleazy old-fashioned farmhouse, the permanency of the good productive earth and all living things. If only he could stay here for ever and be his own man — or Sugar Fossett's man — he'd never crave anything else in his life, or get even a parking ticket from the law. But in despair he realised he would never be his own man again. He belonged to Haldane, the easy murderer, and the resolute desperadoes of the drug-making consortium. And if he went against them they would either kill him, like swatting a fly, or they would send him back to the Scrubs for interminable years.

When their comradeship had developed and prospered for a week or two, Sugar cemented their relationship by inviting Terry up to bed as naturally and forthrightly as she would put a bull to a cow. She called it being covered. Ever since puberty she'd done it when she felt like it with any man she fancied. When her early fears of pregnancy had never materialised, she concluded she must be barren or her tubes were blocked. It was a bit of luck which she made good use of, and she enjoyed herself without inhibition throughout her adolescence and young womanhood. She didn't get so many offers now that she was declining into middle age, but she'd taken a fancy to the energetic, fast-talking Terry and decided to give him the incentive to keep on visiting her.

For the first time in his miserable life Terry was fulfilled and happy. If only . . .

* * *

One fine summer evening after Terry had arrived at Vicar's Hill Farm on his bike and had a good meal of Sugar Fossett's home-cured bacon and eggs, there came the crackle of a car's wheels on the dirt road leading into the farmyard, and a landrover went past the kitchen window to pull up in front of the house.

'My God!' exclaimed Terry, pale with alarm. 'Who the hell's that?'

'Why? What are you worried about?' said Sugar with some amusement. 'It's only an old friend of mine, Alvin Ballsover. He's not going to eat you.'

'But — but — ' stammered Terry, backing guiltily away and looking instinctively for somewhere to hide. 'You never told me you had other men here. Where do I stand then in

131

the pecking order?'

'Don't be silly,' she replied brusquely. 'Just because you're my friend it doesn't shut me off from all my other friends and neighbours. I've known them for an awful long time.'

'To hell with him!' exclaimed Terry, his initial fright changing to anger. 'I don't want to meet him. Being civil to a bloody rival is not my scene.'

'Good Lord, Terry! You're jealous!' she exclaimed with a chuckle of delight. 'You mustn't get too possessive over me. Don't start getting ambitious just because we make it well in bed together. I don't belong to anybody but myself.'

Just then a big hulking figure walked past the kitchen window, and the door opened without a prior knock as if the newcomer had a proprietorial right to walk in whenever he chose.

Alvin Ballsover, estate manager for Aldingbourne Manor, was a big red-faced, blunt-featured countryman dressed for the part in brown tweed hat, brown tweed suit and brown leather gaiters. Aged about forty, he had small close-set eyes entirely disproportionate to his big domineering nose and thick unsmiling lips. He was by nature surly and morose and difficult to get to know. He was also instinctively hostile to anybody who appeared even remotely as a threat to his interests, and Sugar Fossett had been a favourite interest for a long time. He'd been married years ago when he first came to work on the estate, but his young wife was a flighty piece who found life in the country a drag, and her sober, hard-working, thrifty husband a crashing bore. She'd run off with a flashy, facetious electrician who had a good sideline in fixing up the flashing lights at discos. After a lot of unpleasantness Alvin Ballsover got his divorce and had lived alone with increasing moroseness in his cottage on the estate ever since. He decided that if he ever married again it would be only for sound practical and profitable reasons, like forming a merger with a good piece of property so that he wouldn't have to work for that stuffed shirt Carvell any more.

Sugar Fossett, a fine figure of a

woman, a hard worker and reliable friend, possessing her own farm with a hundred good acres was reason enough for any countryman with an eye to the main chance to think of changing his status. Ballsover had been trying to talk her into marriage for some years, but she always put him off with a merry quip, softened by an expression of appreciation in order not to offend him completely. As estate manager for Aldingbourne Manor he was useful to her in all kinds of ways. He sent a vehicle to pick up her daily milk yield and transported it with the Carvell output to the Milk Marketing Centre. When there was a shoot over the Carvell estate with the owner's political and aristocratic guests pouring out death and destruction on the wild life, Alvin Ballsover always saw to it that Sugar Fossett received a couple of brace of pheasant or mallard. When she needed to borrow some expensive mechanised equipment such as a tractor-mounted hedge-cutter or ditch excavator, it only needed a telephone call to Alvin Ballsover. If her beat-up old Morris

Minor estate car wouldn't start, Alvin would drop everything to come over and do a quick fix on her plugs and points.

Obviously she wouldn't have liked to be without him altogether, but she wanted to keep him at arm's length. Once she took him into her farm as a husband, she knew he would take over completely. She and her farm would become his property, and Sugar wouldn't be free any more. She would decline by degrees to the status of a doormat. He would dominate her by brute force if necessary, and he wasn't even fun to be with. She found it a positive strain to sustain a conversation with him, and always felt an easing of tension after he'd gone.

Alvin Ballsover stopped dead in his tracks when he saw Munton in Sugar's kitchen, and the habitual scowl on his big red face grew even darker. Terry was not a prepossessing sight with his slightly built, stoop-shouldered figure, his long lank black hair and unkempt beard. Dressed conventionally in denim jeans, sneakers and T-shirt, he looked to Ballsover like a typical idle unemployable, a scrounger and a parasite. His presence in Sugar's house with the greasy plate and utensils still on the table before him spoke for itself, and the slow build-up of jealous rage began in Alvin Ballsover.

'Hullo, Al,' said Sugar with her usual hearty bonhomie. 'This is Terry, a friend of mine. Terry, this is Alvin Ballsover, estate manager for Mr Carvell.'

The two men just glowered at each other without speaking like a couple of tomcats.

'Terry's a research chemist from London,' went on Sugar as if to justify him. 'He's staying in the country for a rest and a change.'

'Is that a fact?' growled Ballsover suspiciously. 'What! Staying here, in this house?'

'No, of course not. He's with a friend, the new tenant of Woodfield Hollow. You must know about him.'

'Oh, the Rhodesian feller, Haldane. Yes, I know him,' said Ballsover with a grating bark of a laugh. 'A right bloody genius of a farmer he is! From what I've seen and heard as I go about the estate, he's got no more idea how to run a farm than build a spaceship. I suppose him and his type can only make their farms pay in Rhodesia because they've got a big pool of cheap black labour to do all the work, while they sit on their fat arses in the fancy white clubs, drinking sundowners. You can tell him I said so.'

'Don't worry. I'll tell him,' said Terry with equal animosity.

'So you're a research chemist, are you?' went on Ballsover, glowering at him malevolently. 'I suppose it's people like you we've got to thank for all these poisonous weedkillers and insecticides killing everything off and upsetting the balance of nature.'

'I've never worked on a weedkiller in my life,' retorted Terry angrily.

'So what do you work on?'

'New medicines and drugs for the medical profession: safer anaesthetics and pain killers, cures for heart disease and cancer. Pharmaceuticals in other words. You wouldn't understand.'

'What the hell do you mean, I wouldn't

understand? Are you saying I'm too bloody thick to know about drugs?'

'Well, you said it!'

'Oh, for God's sake, you two, don't be so childish!' scolded Sugar. 'What's got into you? It's a pity if I can't invite a couple of men into my kitchen without them snarling at each other like cat and dog.'

'Well, I'm sorry, lass,' growled Ballsover, 'but it just got up my nose seeing him here like a bloody free loader, eating your grub, swilling your beer as if he owns the place. What else of yours is he helping himself to? Or is that getting too personal?'

'Now look here, Al!' exclaimed Sugar indignantly. 'I owe you a lot and I've always made you welcome here, but if you're going to get nasty — '

'All right, all right, lass. Forget I said it,' muttered Ballsover suitably chastened. 'I came to talk to you about borrowing the hay-baler for your top field. When do you want it for?'

'Well, I'd say the grass is in prime condition now,' replied Sugar. 'As long as the weather stays fine you can bring it round any day. Thanks Al. I'll be glad of it.'

They went on to discuss other farming matters, and Terry, feeling left out of it, decided it was time to go. If he stayed any longer he was bound to lose his temper and stick one on Alvin Ballsover, the ugly fat git! Terry was discreet enough to realise that getting into brawls with the local peasantry was a sure way of attracting attention to himself that could be highly dangerous.

'Good night, Terry,' called Sugar as he slunk away. 'Feel free to drop in for a cuppa next time you're passing.'

Terry got on his bike and pedalled off down the lane feeling angry and depressed at the new development. He might have known! Sugar Fossett was too good to be true. A woman with all she had going for her was bound to have some tweedy, bull-and-beef yokel sniffing around, one of her own kind who shared her way of life, eager to marry her and take over the farm. Terry had been a loser all his life, so why should things work out any differently with Sugar Fossett? It looked like the end of his beautiful dream of being there alone with her, enjoying the domesticity he'd always yearned for.

But he wasn't going to give up on her because of Alvin Ballsover. He'd be back regularly for his free grub and nooky. And if it came to the crunch he'd really take care of that big, surly, shit-faced yokel the way Haldane had taken care of that snooper last March. Getting one in first was all that really counted in any conflict.

11

Alvin Ballsover was so upset and alarmed by the advent of the smarmy Londoner into Sugar Fossett's life that he thought about nothing else. If Sugar had taken such a fancy to him, having him in the house at all hours and cooking him meals, it meant she was getting screwed by him as well. As Alvin Ballsover knew to his cost there was no accounting for the bloody-minded perversity of women when they took a shine to some weedy, despicable little rat whose only asset was making them giggle in bed (something which Alvin had never been able to do). If Sugar was hooked on a sponger and a parasite who could move into the farm on a long-term basis and even make it legal, Alvin's long-standing, carefully maturing plan for becoming an owner farmer would come to nothing.

So Ballsover started to observe the comings and goings at Vicar's Hill Farm.

He sat in his Landrover a hundred yards down the road after he'd seen Terry arrive at the farm. He seethed with fury when he saw the light go on in Sugar's bedroom and then go out again. At two o'clock in the morning there was still no sign of Terry emerging from the farm, so there was nothing for it but to go back to his lonely cottage, brooding and apoplectic with a terrible rage. He knew it would be worse than counter-productive to storm in there, haul the interloper out of her bed and smash him to pulp. Sugar would never speak to him again, and Vicar's Hill Farm would be permanently lost. On the other hand it was impossible for him to stand idly by and watch Sugar being made a fool of by that nasty sponging little creep who'd never done an honest day's work in his life. Alvin's jealous fury was building up to the point of insanity.

One evening as he prowled round the country lanes in his Landrover within a two-mile radius of Vicar's Hill Farm on the look-out for his hated rival, suddenly he'd had enough. The sight of the familiar scrawny figure in denim jeans and T-shirt cycling purposefully down the lane to his rendezvous with Sugar caused all restraint to snap in Alvin Ballsover. It was time to teach the creep a real lesson.

As Terry rode towards him Ballsover swung the Landrover to the other side of the road and drove straight at him, accelerating recklessly with murderous intent. Terry yelled out in panic as he swerved desperately onto the verge to avoid the charging vehicle. The front wheel of his bike went down in a rut and the cycle stood on end, catapulting him into the ditch. He landed flat on his belly in the muddy ditch bottom with a thump that winded him.

As he struggled to sit upright, spitting damp earth out of his mouth, he saw the Landrover stop a few yards down the lane. It was flung violently into reverse gear and roared backwards to run over Terry's bike. The front wheel and forks were mangled beyond repair by the fat back wheel of the Landrover. Terry was practically gibbering with fury as Ballsover switched off his motor and lumbered out of the vehicle. He wore a sadistic grin on his big bucolic face and brandished a stout walking stick in his hand.

'You bastard!' yelled Terry. 'You mad stupid bastard! You tried to kill me. It was deliberate.'

'Maybe it was, and maybe I'll have better luck next time,' jeered Ballsover. 'You'd better make sure there's not a next time, see? Stay away from Sugar Fossett.'

'Like hell I will! Who are you to give me orders? She doesn't want you, you bloody gormless peasant! No woman would want you. And as long as she asks me to, I'll go on covering her.'

'Not when I've finished with you, you won't,' snarled Ballsover.

He raised his walking stick and gave Terry a stinging whack across the left arm, which caused him to howl with pain. In a spirited counterstroke Terry launched a savage kick at Ballsover's groin, but the big man easily parried it with his stick and then gave Terry

144

another numbing blow on the same arm.

Terry recoiled, feeling sick with pain, and retreated hastily down the road. Ballsover followed him, mercilessly beating him about the head, shoulders and buttocks with the stick. Racked with pain and in sheer desperation Terry managed to fling himself through a gap in the hedge and squeeze between two strands of barbed wire, where the lumbering, ungainly Ballsover couldn't follow. With the hedge and wire between them the two mortal enemies roared threats and obscenities.

'Stay away from Sugar Fossett!' yelled Ballsover. 'She can't afford to keep a hippy parasite like you. Next time I catch you going there I'll beat your bloody brains out.'

'You dumb yokel!' bawled Terry. 'I'll get you for this. You owe me fifty quid for my bike you just smashed up.'

'Come and take it out on my hide,' jeered Ballsover.

'I'll report you to the fuzz. It's against the law what you just did.'

'Where are your witnesses? Your word

against mine, and I know who the police are more likely to believe.'

After ranting and slanging in similar vein for some time they parted with hatred at fever heat and nothing resolved.

When Ballsover had driven away Terry came back to recover his vandalised bike, and pushed it on its back wheel the rest of the way to Vicar's Hill Farm. Sugar ran out of her kitchen in alarm when she saw the bedraggled, mud-covered scarecrow limping along, supporting the mangled front wheel of his bike, looking like the victim of a road accident.

'Terry!' she cried. 'What happened to you? Oh my dear, what on earth did you run into? Are you all right?'

'It was him who ran into me,' declared Terry venomously. 'That bloody friend of yours, Ballsover. And it was no accident.'

'What! Alvin? I don't believe it. He wouldn't harm anybody deliberately. Why should he?'

'Jealousy,' retorted Terry. 'Crude old-fashioned jealousy. This was his way of warning me off. Is he your husband or something?'

146

'No, of course not.'

'Well, he's acting like it. He thinks you're his private property, He told me to stay away from you or he'd beat my brains out. He battered me with a club. See these weals? He swore he'd kill me next time I came here.'

'My God!' muttered Sugar. She was sincerely shocked by this brutal evidence of Ballsover's violence, but being a woman she was not entirely displeased at the gladiatorial combat over her person.

'What on earth could have got into the man? I had no idea he had those ideas about me. I shall have to have words with him over this.'

'You do that,' said Terry savagely. 'But you'd better catch him fast while he's still in one piece, because I'm going to get the bastard for this. I'll murder the fat swine, no matter what they do to me after.'

Sugar Fossett saw the glint of sheer naked evil in his eye and was momentarily terrified.

'No, Terry, please!' she implored. 'Don't talk like that. You can't win by more violence. It'll only land you in trouble.'

'Trouble!' he exclaimed bitterly, pointing to the mud plastered all over his clothes and the ugly purple weals left by Ballsover's stick. 'Am I supposed to put up with this kind of treatment every time I come to see you? He started it, but by God, I'm going to finish it.'

'No, Terry,' she said firmly. 'This childish feud goes no farther. I insist. If you want to see me again you've got to promise me you won't try to hurt Alvin. I shall get the same promise from him. If the two of you must behave like wild animals to each other, it won't be for my sake because I shan't see or speak to either of you again. Do I get your promise? I mean it, Terry.'

'All right,' he muttered reluctantly, knowing that promises are only made to be kept while convenient. 'But you'd better get it through Ballsover's thick head as well. He tried to kill me on my bike, so he really means it.'

'Don't worry. I'll make sure that Alvin keeps the peace as well,' she assured him

148

confidently. 'Now come on inside and let's clean you up a bit. I never saw anybody in such a mess.'

'You mean we can take a bath together?' he said eagerly.

'Why not, if it'll put you in a better frame of mind?'

★ ★ ★

Having been duly scolded by Sugar for his loutish attack on her friend Terry, and having given her his reluctant promise to call a truce, Ballsover was constrained to keep the peace. But there was still murderous fury in his heart over Terry's continuing success with Sugar Fossett. He watched from a concealed vantage point as Terry cycled up to Vicar's Hill Farm on his new bike two or three times a week, and stayed the night till Sugar got up with the dawn.

Although the direct physical attack had been forbidden by his lady, Ballsover could still look around for some more subtle and underhand way to do Terry a mischief, and hopefully banish him from

Sugar Fossett's arms. Perhaps there was some dubious factor in the set-up at Woodfield Hollow which could be turned to advantage in making trouble for Terry. So Ballsover often found the time, while doing his rounds of the estate, to park his Landrover in a clump of trees on a hill half-a-mile away and looked down at the farm in the hollow through a pair of binoculars.

Although he was general overseer of the estate and attended to such matters as the game preserves for shooting, the culverts and land drainage, and re-letting a farm when the tenants left, it wasn't within his brief to interfere in the general running of the Carvell tenant farms. But Ballsover had a sharp eye as to what was being done or left undone all over the five-thousand acre estate. He knew who the efficient, hard-working farmers were, and who were the feckless, shiftless husbandmen who couldn't make a go of it even on government subsides and EEC guaranteed prices. He'd noticed how Woodfield Hollow had been running down fast since the Rhodesian Haldane took it over in the preceding September. He'd been gradually running down the livestock over the winter months so that he now had no pigs at all and only a couple of cows and a dozen hens for domestic use. There had been no planting of cereal or root crops in the autumn or spring, so that there were sixty good acres of high yielding arable land lying fallow.

Haldane wasn't interested in making money from the farm. He was just living there, having paid the year's rent in advance, which must be a total loss. What was his game? Was he using the farm as a front, and if so, for what?

As he sulked and brooded over it Ballsover suddenly remembered the well-dressed, smooth talking stranger who'd button-holed him in The Lord Burleigh last summer, plied him generously with whisky and asked him about farm tenancies falling vacant on the Carvell estate. He'd seemed really excited at the news that the Pykes were clearing out of Woodfield Hollow and it would be vacant in September.

Ballsover had attached no significance whatsoever to the encounter until Mr Carvell had come up to the Manor during the Parliamentary summer recess, and had made a special visit to Ballsover's cottage to ask him if he'd re-let Woodfield Hollow yet. As it happened Ballsover had promised the tenancy to an old friend of his who was farming in a poor way in Norfolk. But Digby Carvell had promptly scotched that little project. He'd insisted brusquely with no argument that the farm be let to a Rhodesian farmer who'd been forced out of his own country and deserved a fresh start.

Ballsover didn't like being made a fool of, or being reviled as a Judas by his former friend. He'd wondered at the time with futile rage what kind of bent and devious skulduggery was going on between his employer and the tall, villainous-looking Rhodesian, Henry Haldane, but he supposed resignedly that he'd never find out.

With the unfolding realisation that Haldane was a sham farmer who had no interest in agriculture, and now that the seedy Londoner imposing on Sugar Fossett was also involved with him, Ballsover's malicious interest in Woodfield Hollow quickened into an obsession. He desperately wanted to know what was going on there. He spent nearly as much time crouched in the hilltop copse, examining Woodfield Hollow through his binoculars, as he spent in watching Terry's evening visits to Sugar Fossett.

As far as Ballsover could tell, the only place where there seemed to be any activity at Woodfield Hollow was in the pre-fabricated concrete structure next to the old cattle byre which had been added as a milking shed and used as such by the previous tenant.

Under the Haldane regime the two surviving cows were never taken in there for milking. The scrawny little rat called Terry, the self-styled research chemist, seemed to spend most of his day in there, dressed in a white lab coat as if the former milking parlour really was a laboratory. The tall figure of Haldane dressed in his khaki drill slacks and tunic style bush shirt also went in and out from time to time as if in a supervisory capacity.

On one occasion Ballsover saw Haldane return to the farm in his dark blue estate car, and start unloading a lot of plastic carrier bags filled to capacity with something unidentifiable. Terry in his white coat came out and helped him to carry them inside the concrete building. On another day the reverse process was in operation. The bulky white plastic bags were brought out of the shed and loaded into Haldane's car by the two men. Haldane then drove away alone and wasn't seen for the rest of the day.

Ballsover's simple deduction from all this was that some raw material was being taken into the concrete building and a finished product was coming out. Haldane handled the transport end of it and Terry, working inside all day, must be concerned with the manufacturing process. So if Terry really was a research chemist, then the stuff going into the lab must be the raw chemicals from which some finished chemical product

154

was being made and then disposed of by Haldane.

Alvin Ballsover was not an imaginative man, but his hatred of Sugar Fossett's new friend now caused his reasoning powers to make a real leap forward. One thing for sure, they wouldn't be making weedkiller or insecticide or fertiliser in there. The quantities of materials involved were far too small to be viable, when the stuff could be produced in bulk far more economically by ICI than by some do-it-yourself chemist in a backyard laboratory. Hadn't Terry said something about pharmaceuticals, drugs and medicine for the medical profession, something which he, Alvin Ballsover, was far too thick to know about?

Drugs!

That was the emotive word, the scourge of mankind. Ballsover had read enough about it in the newspapers and watched enough drug sagas on television to know that peddling drugs was the most lucrative form of criminal exploitation. Smuggling drugs into the country was a spectacular, multi-million pound business, but far less was heard of the drugs which were home-made, produced in small, illicit laboratories in this country and put straight on the home market without running the gauntlet of Customs officers or police at the ports and airfields. Come to think of it, that Terry looked like a shifty little criminal type, evil enough for anything, and the Rhodesian Haldane, bogus farmer, looked like a real cut-throat.

Though Ballsover himself wasn't particularly virtuous or respectful of the law, he saw the possibility of illicit drug-making at Woodfield Hollow as a lever to get rid of Terry and Haldane; above all to remove Terry far away forever from Sugar Fossett's welcoming arms. He wanted to be sure of his ground. He longed to get a look inside that prefabricated structure where Terry spent so many hours each day. He wouldn't have minded chancing his arm by snooping round there after Haldane had driven off for the day with a load of the mysterious product. But through his binoculars he'd also spotted the dog

Angus slinking round the outbuildings, a big black and brown villainous looking cur, either Doberman or Rotweiler, that would tear any trespasser limb from limb. Ballsover wasn't brave or foolhardy enough to take that on.

He thought about reporting his suspicions to the police, but his own experiences with the local constabulary hadn't been such as to promote either liking or trust. When he'd caught a couple of lads stealing his pheasants in the Carvell woods, the police had advised him to drop the case. There wasn't enough evidence, they said: Ballsover's word against the lads, who were denying it strenuously. It was a waste of time and public money to bring such an unsubstantiated case before the Justices, who would give the police a roasting for pursuing it.

Ballsover could well imagine how those dim woodentop wollies would laugh him right out of the nick if he went there to report an illicit drugs factory at Woodfield Hollow Farm. What evidence did he have? He'd be told to mind his own business and not waste police time. However, he soon cheered up at the realisation that there was another way to stir things up if there were any illegal practices going on at Woodfield Hollow. He'd throw it all in the lap of his employer, the celebrated Digby Carvell, MP. As minister of the Crown he certainly wouldn't want any criminal activity on one of his farms to be made known. Whatever corrupt favouritism he'd been prepared to show to Haldane, he couldn't condone or cover up a drugs scandal, especially when Ballsover suggested calling in the police. Haldane and his unsavoury stable mate would have to clear right out of Woodfield Hollow, right out of the country in order to save Carvell's political career and reputation. There could be no question as to where Carvell's priorities would lie. That was Alvin Ballsover's hard-headed assessment of the position, and he liked it very much.

He was so sure he was right that he telephoned his employer at his flat in Park Lane, something he'd never dared do before, for Carvell had always made it clear to his estate manager that he didn't want to be bothered with petty domestic details on the estate while he was in London absorbed in his Parliamentary and ministerial duties. Ballsover was paid to take overall responsibility for all problems that might arise.

He rang the Park Lane number at ten o'clock at night, but there was no reply. He rang again just after midnight, but Digby was still out on the town as it behoved a dynamic young minister. So Ballsover rang him up at seven o'clock next morning when he came back to his cottage after his customary first inspection of the Manor Farm.

Digby, having been in bed for only two hours after a mammoth *soirée* and making it with a new love at the American Embassy was less than pleased at being shattered out of a deep sleep so early.

'Mr Carvell, sir. It's Alvin Ballsover here. I have to talk to you. It's very urgent.'

'Ballsover!' spluttered Digby with mounting indignation as he came awake.

'Haven't I told you not to pester me here? I do *not* mix my domestic life with my political career. Now is that finally understood?'

'Understood sir,' said Ballsover, his thick lips curling in an unpleasant sneer. Most English workers hate and despise their boss, especially if he sits a layer or two above them in the social stratification and talks with a pretentious accent. Ballsover was no exception.

'Dammit, man!' raged Digby. 'I pay you enough to take relevant decisions for the running of the estate — '

'Beg pardon, sir,' interposed Ballsover implacably, 'but this is not about the estate, not in a normal manner of speaking. I think there's summat going on that's not right, and you ought to know about it.'

'What's that?' exclaimed Digby with a sudden icy shock of foreboding. 'You're making no sense, man. What isn't right?'

'It's him that you insisted on putting into Woodfield Hollow last September: Haldane.'

'What about Haldane?' said Digby,

growing even colder.

'Begging your pardon, sir, but he's the lousiest farmer I ever saw. He's running that farm right down into nothing. There's been no ploughing or sowing done this year. The whole piece of arable land is lying fallow. He should never have been allowed anywhere near a farm. It's going to take years to get the land back into condition again. Now if we'd stayed with the tenant I recommended — '

'Ballsover,' said Digby haughtily, 'you're boring me. You're the estate manager, and if you see something badly wrong with a farm — '

'But he can't be making a penny out of that farm, sir. I reckon he's using it as a front for summat else.'

'Good God, man!' said Digby, starting to sweat. 'What nonsense! How can you know that?'

'I got eyes, sir, as I go about the estate. Haldane has got another feller living at the farm with him, a Londoner called Terry. I never did get to hear his other name. He looks like a dropout, says he's a research chemist. They've got summat going on in the new milking shed. I've seen the Londoner coming out of there wearing a white coat.'

'Perhaps he wears it to milk the cows,' said Digby shrilly.

'Not on your life, sir. There's never a cow goes in that shed. Haldane himself milks 'em in the old byre. I reckon they're making summat in that milking shed that doesn't have much to do with farming. I've seen Haldane and this Terry unload a carful of plastic bags, filled with what could be some kind of powder. Then they bring out the same plastic bags, still full. They load them in the car and Haldane drives away.'

'But it's their own business, and I certainly don't want to be pestered with it,' cried Digby, desperately trying to control his fear. 'Allow me to remind you, Ballsover, that you're not paid to spend an inordinate amount of time spying on the comings and goings of one indifferent farmer, who probably has other interests.'

'With respect, sir, it's your business and mine if something illegal is going on at Woodfield Hollow,' persisted Ballsover stoutly. 'Just suppose they're making drugs there, like Notensil, that stuff the racecourse gangs use for nobbling the favourite in a big race. Well, that man Terry says he's a research chemist who works in pharmaceuticals after all. And they keep a bloody big savage dog there — looks like a Doberman — so nobody can sneak up and have a look. When it all comes out, sir, that it's been happening on your property, with or without your say-so, it's not going to do your reputation any good, or mine for that matter. In fact they'd try to make out I'd connived at it and was an accessory. So I reckon to clear ourselves we ought to call in the police. Let them check out what's being done in the new milking shed at Woodfield. And if it turns out to be summat harmless, there won't be any bones broken, will there?'

'Yes, yes, I see what you mean, Ballsover,' said Digby, his panic-stricken mind working at high speed to find a way out of this mess. 'I appreciate your concern, of course. Thank you for being so frank. But if you don't mind I'd rather you didn't call in the police at your end.'

'Why not, sir?'

'It only needs an incautious leak to the press — you know what these country bobbies are — and my whole position as a minister might be irrevocably damaged. Leave it with me, Ballsover.'

'Well, I understand that, sir. But the matter ought to be looked into. We can't just let it go and hope there's nothing illegal being done there.'

'Of course not, and I've absolutely no intention of doing that. I shall look into this matter myself. I intend to make a special journey up to the estate and confront Haldane myself. I shall demand to see whatever is being done inside the milking shed you refer to. If it should prove to be something, as you say, illegal, I shall inform Scotland Yard myself. It will need the real experts to deal with a situation as delicate as this.'

'Well, that's fair enough, sir,' conceded Ballsover with deep satisfaction. 'But might I ask how soon you'll be going to see Haldane? I appreciate you're a busy man at Westminster and all that. But this Woodfield Hollow business can't be put off. It could break out into a full-blown scandal any day.'

'Don't worry, Ballsover. I realise the urgency of this situation probably better than you do. Leave it till the weekend when I shall be free to come up there and deal with it. I need hardly remind you of the utmost confidentiality in this affair. Not a word about it to anyone else.'

'I understand, sir,' said Ballsover. 'You can depend on me.'

He put the phone down and rubbed his hands in triumph. His thick lips broke into a complacent grin.

'Give it a week,' he told himself, 'and Terry the chemist will be either in gaol or on the run. In any case he won't be sweetening up Sugar Fossett any more.'

12

While Alvin Ballsover's machinations against him gathered momentum, Terry was also scheming to get his revenge on the estate manager who had beaten him like a dog. If he followed his inclination to waylay Ballsover outside his cottage one night and beat his head in with a blunt instrument, Sugar would know immediately who the culprit was. Not only would she carry out her threat to give Terry the elbow, she might also feel it her duty to tip off the police about someone with a good reason for scrambling Ballsover's brains. That was a risk Terry dare not even contemplate. He had to work out some devious and cunning stroke to inflict injury on Ballsover in such a way that nobody could be sure it was foul play, or suspect that Terry had had a hand in it.

He soon came up with the idea of administering LSD to his enemy so that

Ballsover, in the throes of a devastating trip and not knowing what was happening to him, would do something wildly outrageous like trying to fly over a tree in his Landrover, or raping the Lady Lucinda up at the Manor.

Terry set to work in his lab while manufacturing his usual quota of micro-dots, and made up a hundred tablets disguised as aspirin tablets, each of which contained three times the dose of the hallucinogenic contained in a microdot. Then he made a discreet reconnaissance of Aldingbourne Manor and found out that Ballsover lived alone in the old lodge-keeper's cottage beside the huge ornate wrought-iron gates of the Manor approach road. It was a single-storey Victorian Gothic cottage, stoutly built from grey blocks of Colly Weston stone. It had tall spiral chimneys like sticks of barley sugar, a steeply pitched stone slab roof, and narrow ogival windows that looked a bit like the weapon slits in a medieval fortress. It looked wildly picturesque and romantic, but inside it was dark and damp with no mains gas and with its water supplied by a deep well in the back yard.

Terry waited concealed in the surrounding rhododendron bushes one evening until he saw Ballsover drive away in his Landrover, probably to maintain his jealous surveillance on Vicar's Hill Farm. Round the back of the cottage Terry's experienced eye soon spotted a vulnerable sash window whose catch could be sprung without damage by the blade of a knife.

In a few seconds Terry had raised the sash and vaulted over the window sill into the cottage. He found himself in Ballsover's bedroom with its rumpled, unmade bed and dirty socks and shoes all over the place, the typical squalid flea-pit of a man long used to living alone. In fact the whole cottage was a sleazy tip with dust lying thick on old-fashioned, inelegant furniture, and dirty crockery filling the stained kitchen sink. It stank of stale tobacco, old clothes and beer. No wonder Ballsover wanted to promote himself to Vicar's Hill Farm with Sugar Fossett to look after him.

In the primitive bathroom which was

like a dingy, brown-painted ninteenth century museum, Terry homed in on the crude old medicine cabinet, hanging on the wall above the throne, which contained Ballsover's shaving gear, a bottle of Grecian 2000 which he used to encourage his thinning hair, and two brown medicine bottles containing pills. One held tablets of Dulcolax which he used periodically for his bouts of constipation. The other was a bottle of aspirin, half-full, which Ballsover needed for his morning hangover when he'd been drowning his sorrows too earnestly at The Lord Burleigh.

Swiftly Terry seized on the aspirin bottle, flushed its contents down the lavatory and replaced them with an equal number of the bogus, LSD-intensive aspirins of his own manufacture. Then he silently withdrew, carefully closing the sash window behind him.

★ ★ ★

After the unnerving call from his estate manager Digby Carvell was in a permanent state of fear. He could see the whole of his brilliant career and his future of wealth and privilege coming to pieces in his hands. Thanks to that damned, diabolical woman Elaine Cornford who'd delivered him bound hand and foot to her villainous husband, he was now head over heels into a criminal conspiracy. Alvin Ballsover could be wrong about the nefarious activity at Woodfield Hollow, but that was a very slender hope. There was every likelihood that Carrington and his fellow criminals had sited an illicit drugs plant on the Carvell Estate. Digby himself could hardly evade responsibility when it became known that he'd over-ruled Ballsover to install Haldane at Woodfield Hollow.

He had only three days grace to remove the appalling threat to his future. He couldn't trust Ballsover not to go to the police unless Digby appeared on the estate by the weekend and convinced him either that Haldane was doing nothing illegal, or that Haldane had been sent packing from Woodfield Hollow, with Scotland Yard fully in the picture.

Digby needed desperately to get hold of Carrington and warn him to wind up and obliterate whatever crooked practises he and Haldane had in progress at Woodfield Hollow.

Digby had no means of communicating with Carrington except through Elaine, and he didn't ever want to see her again. Relations between them had been glacial since that awful day when she'd set him up to be her crooked husband's puppet. But fear had a greater pull than pride, so in the intervals between busy committees during the morning Digby found time to telephone Elaine at her Chelsea home.

'Oh, hullo darling,' she gushed in her professionally seductive voice. 'How nice to hear from you again.'

'That's not my feeling,' he replied stonily. 'I have to see you at once. Are you at home today?'

'But of course, darling. I'm always at home to a minister of the Crown. When may I expect the pleasure?'

'In an hour's time,' he snarled, and slammed the phone down.

Elaine was in her Grecian gown,

touching-in the pastoral background of the life-size portrait of a distinguished City banker. She put down her palette and brush and shimmered across the room to greet him with outstretched hands.

'My dear, why have you left it so long? Friendships should be kept in constant repair.'

'Don't talk to me about friendship,' he retorted savagely. 'I have to speak to your husband urgently. I take it you're still in touch?'

'But of course.'

'Where can I reach him?'

'Dear Digby, you look so harassed and fraught. Do sit down and have a drink.'

'I've every reason to be harassed and fraught,' he stormed. 'Thanks to you and your blackmail conspiracy, my whole future is threatened. That precious husband of yours and his villainous friends have set up an illegal drugs factory on one of the farms on my estate.'

'No! Digby, what are you saying? I'm sure you must be mistaken,' she cried,

172

her eyes wide with disbelief.

'There's no mistake. My estate manager has seen enough to make him very suspicious, and he wants to go to the police. I've managed to talk him out of it for a couple of days, but the whole criminal business must be closed down and every trace removed by the weekend. Otherwise the Drugs Squad will be knocking on my door, and I shall have to refer them to your husband.'

'Oh, Digby,' she gushed, 'you're so dramatic, melodramatic, in fact. I think you must be exaggerating. Donald would never allow himself to be caught up in anything so dangerous.'

'Don't be stupid!' he exclaimed roughly. 'That was the whole purpose behind that sordid little trap you prepared for me, so that he could bury me under scandal and disgrace if I refused to co-operate.'

'Digby, I swear I never knew anything about that,' she protested, 'and I don't want to know now. I'm quite content to leave you strong, clever men to do your wheeling and dealing, scoring points off each other, without involving me.'

'So you just want to be the little woman after all,' he sneered, 'and you don't object to a cheap criminal for your lord and master. Elaine, I've got to talk to him immediately. You'd better convince him that he's got to move fast, or we'll all be standing in the dock. Don't think your part in the conspiracy will go unpunished.'

Elaine, now somewhat devoid of her usual cool serenity, went into her boudoir to make a phone-call to her husband, as a result of which Digby returned to her house the same evening for a stormy and acrimonious meeting with Donald Carrington.

★ ★ ★

On Friday night Alvin Ballsover was in The Lord Burleigh at Aldingbourne village according to his weekly routine. He always reckoned to finish off the working week with a skinful, which helped to put him in a better frame of mind. On Saturday morning he would go shooting over the estate to bag a few brace of mallard. The afternoon he would spend at Vicar's Hill Farm doing odd jobs round the house for Sugar Fossett and generally oiling his way round her to drive home his invariable message that she really needed a man's permanent attendance on the farm.

It made him feel even better to know that after this coming weekend when the big bust-up came with those crooks at Woodfield Hollow, his hated rival wouldn't be around any more to corrupt Sugar Fossett.

At ten-thirty when he'd drunk his quota Ballsover growled his usual gruff goodnight to the landlord and shambled outside to his vehicle. It had only recently got completely dark, and the residual heat of the summer's day was still hanging in the still air, radiating from the grey stone walls of the old pub. There were at least a dozen customers' vehicles still parked in the open parking space at one side of the pub, and Ballsover didn't give a second glance to the large dark saloon that was drawn up behind his Landrover.

As he fumbled unsteadily with his

key a large black figure materialised silently out of the night behind him. The edge of a hand came violently down in a swift, paralysing Karate chop to the side of Ballsover's fleshy neck. Consciousness exploded and died. As his knees sagged the assailant caught him round the waist in a powerful embrace and dragged him to the back door of the dark saloon. He heaved Ballsover's inert bulk unceremoniously onto the backseat, climbed in behind the wheel and drove quickly away. There were no witnesses. The whole operation had taken only a few seconds. Alvin Ballsover was never seen again. There was only his abandoned Landrover in the pub car park to testify that The Lord Burleigh had been his last calling place on that Friday night.

★ ★ ★

When Digby Carvell heard of the unaccountable disappearance of his estate manager from a normal Friday night's drinking session at the village pub, he felt sick with a terrible fear that he didn't want to face up to. The one indisputable fact he latched on to was that the immediate threat of Ballsover making trouble about Woodfield Hollow had been mercifully removed. That in itself was a great relief. But behind it loomed the dreadful uncertainty as to what had really happened to Ballsover. Where could he have gone? Was he still alive? How had he been spirited away from The Lord Burleigh, leaving his Landrover in the pub car park?

The local police were being tight-lipped in their press releases, though a senior officer of the Northamptonshire Constabulary had admitted that foul play couldn't be entirely ruled out.

Digby craved reassurance that the awful suspicion dawning in his mind was unfounded, that Ballsover's disappearance had nothing to do with his own warning to Carrington about the estate manager's snooping round what he suspected to be a drugs farm. Digby tried to contact Elaine Cornford to insist on another urgent meeting with her husband, but

Elaine wasn't answering the telephone. When he went round to her Chelsea house it was closed up and apparently uninhabited. The next door neighbour thought she was out of town, probably on holiday. In sheer desperation Digby motored down to Brighton to the house in the Regency square where he'd first been confronted by Elaine's husband. But that too was empty and closed up. Nobody in the neighbourhood could tell him when Carrington had last been there, or where he'd gone.

In mounting panic Digby considered travelling up to Northamptonshire to confront Haldane at Woodfield Hollow and insist on inspecting the farm to satisfy himself that Ballsover's suspicions had been unfounded. But now the fear amounting to certitude was so great that he shrunk from the final proof about Woodfield Hollow and the fate which had befallen Ballsover. Although he'd never met Henry Haldane, Carrington's Rhodesian nominee, Digby had a deep instinctive dread of the man. It wasn't too melodramatic to suppose that if he went prying round Woodfield Hollow and confronted Haldane with his illicit activity in the milking shed, he might well meet the same fate as Ballsover.

On the other hand, if he reported his suspicions to the police, and the evil conspiracy was uncovered on one of the Aldingbourne tenant farms, he could be virtually sure that Carrington, out of sheer malice, would reveal Digby's own initial connivance and drag him down in the criminal proceedings. In the circumstances therefore, it was best to say nothing, to sit tight with his terrible secrets and hope that nothing would ever come to light about the Carrington/Haldane villainy and what had happened to Alvin Ballsover. Maybe in time they would finish their business at Woodfield Hollow and just go away out of his life.

13

On the Saturday evening Terence Munton had just completed his daily eight-hour shift in the milking shed and produced his daily quota of microdots. It was satisfying creative work, stimulated by the knowledge of how much more cash was coming his way as commission on the day's production.

Haldane had been away from the farm for the past two days, doubtless on his own underhand business. This was why Terry felt so much more relaxed and free and more like a human being now that he had his deeply satisfying love life to look forward to.

It was true that Haldane didn't interfere much with Terry or muck him about, allowing him to do the job in his own way as long as he produced results. But the Rhodesian's mere presence on the farm was uncomfortable and intimidating, reminding Terry automatically of that night of terror and violent death last March, when he'd had a true insight into the real Haldane. Terry still felt irrational stirrings of guilt and fear when Haldane's morose, brooding eyes settled on him with contemptuous disapproval.

Although they lived side by side in the farmhouse and had meals together with a certain accommodation, there'd never been the slightest rapport or cordiality or bridging of the social and human chasm between them. Haldane's whole attitude towards Terry enshrined his remorseless conviction that Munton was an escaped criminal, the lowest dregs of the human heap, who could be dumped back on the garbage tip of Wormwood Scrubs where he belonged as soon as he stepped out of line or ceased to be useful. To Haldane Terry was a white kaffir, just down from the trees and barely human, who would behave himself only as long as his superior cracked the whip.

For his part Terry sullenly resented his leader's heavy arrogance, his bullying assumption of social, moral and racial supremacy. If Haldane was typical of the white tribe of chauvinistic supermen who'd lorded it over Rhodesia, it was small wonder that the disenfranchised and menial blacks had fought a bloody guerrilla war for seven years to get the white royalty down in the earthy arena, where all men's blood and sweat taste the same.

As he was in his bedroom tarting himself up with aftershave and deodorant for his visit to Vicar's Hill Farm and a night's workout with Sugar Fossett, Terry suddenly heard the urgent crunch of tyres on the hard-baked earth of the farm track, and Haldane's large Datsun came swinging in through the gate in a cloud of dust.

'Bugger him!' thought Terry with his usual feeling of unease, insecurity and depression at the approach of Haldane. 'Why the hell couldn't the murdering bastard stay away for a few more days? Who needs the ugly, red-necked swine?'

As Terry came down the narrow staircase into the kitchen Haldane was already crashing through the outer door with a kind of suppressed fury manifest in his every movement. His face was screwed up in a grim, ferocious scowl as he fixed his piercing eyes on the quailing Terry. It was similar to the expression he'd worn that night with the neck of the shattered whisky bottle in his hand and the intruder dead at his feet.

'Munton, you scum! So you had to go shooting your mouth off, you little shit!' he snarled. 'Who else have you bragged to about being a research chemist?'

'Who? Me?' exclaimed Munton desperately. 'I don't know what you mean, guv. I've not told anybody I'm a research chemist.'

'What about the Aldingbourne Manor estate manager, Ballsover? He talked when I put the screw on him. He said you told him you were a research chemist, and that's what gave him the idea we had a drugs factory here.'

Terry went cold with terror as he realised the implications.

'You mean he knows about us here? Where is he then? Has he put the bubble in?'

'No, but it's no thanks to you. He

183

was going to bring in the coppers, but we just managed to get to him first after a tip-off.'

'Ballsover's dead then?'

'What do you think? But it's still touch and go whether we have to shut down the whole operation here if you've told anybody else your bloody trade.'

'But I haven't!' protested Terry vehemently.

'So you say. But who in his right mind is going to believe a little gaol-rat like you?'

His eyes narrowed to such a murderous squint that Terry felt as if they were shrivelling him up. He started to quake with fear.

'You realise what this means, don't you?' went on Haldane savagely. 'It means I can't trust you out of my sight. You're a walking disaster. I'd need somebody else here to watch you round the clock while I was away delivering the microdots. It means you'd have to be locked up here. No more roaming round the countryside on your bike, chatting up peasants like Ballsover and boasting about who you are. You might just as well be back in stir.'

'No, guv'nor, not that! For God's sake don't do that!' pleaded Terry in a panic. 'I'll do anything you say. I'd rather stay here making microdots and never talk to anybody. I swear to God I'll just stay here on the farm, just the same when you're away as when you're here.'

'Oh yes,' sneered Haldane. 'You'd even sign a bit of paper to make it legal! We had a prosperous business going here. We could all have been millionaires in a year or two. But now it's all up the spout, thanks to you! If Ballsover could work it out from talking to you, there must be others you've bragged to who've added it up right. So how long would you say we've got before a whisper gets to some nosey copper out for promotion?'

'Oh, come on, guv,' pleaded Terry desperately. 'It's not as bad as that. Ballsover's the only one.'

'I've told you often enough, Munton. You're expendable. There are plenty of crooked, out-of-work chemists who'd jump at the job and the pay you've got here. So whether we close down the operation or not, you're finished.'

'OK, guv. Anything you say,' said Terry abjectly. 'But give me a sporting chance. Don't just hand me back to the law. Let me disappear. You owe me that. I've worked well for you here the last nine months, haven't I? It doesn't have to be the Scrubs, does it?'

'No, it doesn't have to be the Scrubs,' replied Haldane with an evil grin. 'Wherever you go you'll be ratting on us, buying yourself a better deal from the fuzz by telling them all that's been going on here; tipping them off about that stiff buried up in the woods and putting the finger on me.'

'No, guv! You got me wrong. I'd never do that. I've never grassed anybody in my life.'

'Maybe not, but I'll make bloody sure you don't start with me!' swore Haldane venomously.

He bent down swiftly, pulled up the trouser leg of his KD slacks and snatched from its sheath a wicked-looking, two-edged combat knife, bloodied in many a kaffir during his long and merciless war in the bush.

Terry knew he was a dead man if he didn't move fast. Because he was small he'd always had to be very sharp and quick with instant reflexes in order to survive the savage prison environment without lasting injuries. As the big Rhodesian came at him with his knife, Terry took the only way out. With his head down and his arms clasped tightly over his face for protection, he leapt nimbly up on the draining board and dived headlong at the old decrepit sash window in the kitchen. His momentum carried him clean through it in a shower of disintegrating glass and broken struts. He felt an initial jarring shock on impact, and his arms were cut superficially in many places by slivers of glass. Then he landed on his hands and knees in a thick bed of nettles and burdock, and in one nimble rebound he was up and running for his life.

In anticipation of such a hasty departure from Woodfield Hollow Terry had spent long months in making friends with

Angus the Doberman, feeding him prime steaks and offal from the freezer when Haldane was away, so that the hound was not so incorruptible in his duties as Haldane liked to kid himself. As Angus suddenly appeared round a corner of the cowshed he recognised his friend and romped along beside Terry with playful woofs as he bolted for the woods.

When they reached the far hedge of the first field, Angus whined disconsolately, dropped behind and then went trotting back to meet Haldane who was lumbering vainly in pursuit. Terry clawed his way frenziedly through a gap in the hedge and sprinted on, sheer terror giving fuel to his limbs and breathing. When he'd run more than a mile across country and Haldane had fallen out of sight, Terry paused a few moments to get his breath back. He knew that Haldane hadn't given up even though he was temporarily outstripped. He would never feel safe as long as Terry was alive with all his devastating knowledge about Haldane's crimes. He would use the dog to follow the fugitive's scent wherever it might lead across country. Therefore

Terry had to find himself a set of wheels to break the spoor and put a considerable distance between himself and Woodfield Hollow.

After three more miles of walking and running he came to a 'B' road leading into a grey stone village with a pub called The Curlew. There were cars, motor bikes and pedal bikes strewn carelessly all round the building as the sweating countryfolk slaked their summer thirst. Round the back of the pub Terry found a bicycle which wasn't chained down, and, wheeling it unobtrusively into the road, he pedalled away. Sweating profusely and parched with thirst he reached the outskirts of Kettering as it was getting dark. His clothes were dirty and dishevelled, his fore-arms caked with dried blood from the cuts he'd sustained in crashing through the window, but nobody gave him more than a second glance as he queued up for some fish and chips and cans of orange drink at a jazzy little shop that stayed open to catch the pub trade at closing time.

It was then he realised that he'd only

got a few quid on him. The rest of his ready cash and his Building Society pass books, all the wealth he'd salted away from his prosperous months of making microdots, were hidden in his bedroom at Woodfield Hollow. He'd prised up one of the old floorboards and hidden it in a recess between the joists, for as a working villain he'd always known better than to leave his hard-earned money in some place easily accessible to a casual thief. He hadn't got enough ready cash for his trainfare to London, nor for a night at a hotel. So he had to cycle back into the countryside and sleep in a wayside barn amid the rustlings of sundry vermin. He was still far too shaken by the close call he'd had with Haldane and his knife to contemplate returning to Woodfield Hollow to collect his money.

14

He awoke to hear the church bells ringing in a nearby country church, and realised it was Sunday. Another long hot summer day with nothing to do and nowhere to go, and the certain knowledge that a homicidal Rhodesian maniac would be scouring the countryside with the express purpose of cutting his throat. It didn't take Terry long to remember that he had only one friend left in the world: Sugar Fossett at Vicar's Hill Farm. She would give him food and shelter and maybe even lend him money to get back to the Smoke. He considered the risk that Haldane might know all about Sugar Fossett through his interrogation of Ballsover, in which case Haldane would be watching the farm and waiting for Terry to show up there. On the other hand maybe Ballsover had died without mentioning the Sugar Fossett connection.

It was a fifty-fifty chance but one he couldn't pass up in his present predicament. Unlike Haldane he was no good at living off the land like a savage. Without Sugar's help he had two clear choices: either to die of starvation or surrender to the police.

Still using his stolen bike he made a long detour round the country lanes, following the signposts back to Aldingbourne village, from which he knew his way to Sugar's farm. He kept an apprehensive look-out for Haldane's dark blue Datsun, ready to leap off his bike and take to the woods again, but fortunately there was no sign of his enemy.

By late morning he was crouching in a coppice half-a-mile from Vicar's Hill Farm, watching it anxiously for any sign of unusual visitors or strange vehicles. But the farm lay drowsing in the noon-day heat, presenting its usual image of timeless security and innocence to the strife-battered Munton. The only sign of life was Sugar Fossett in her open-necked shirt and faded jeans going about her daily chores, feeding the hens and carrying swill to the pigs.

Keeping a low profile Munton made a wide circuit of the farm and examined it from every angle. By sundown he was satisfied that neither Haldane nor any other visitor was at the farm, so he decided to risk an approach.

Sugar was in the kitchen making the bedtime cocoa when Terry's face suddenly appeared at the window, dirty and scratched with briars, with bits of straw caught up in his hair and beard. She stared at him in shock and nearly shot her saucepan of milk all over the Aga.

'Can I come in?' he pleaded. 'I'm knackered.'

'You look it,' she retorted. 'Terry, what one earth has happened? Are you in trouble?'

'Not so as you'd notice,' he replied wearily. 'But I'm bloody starving. I could eat a horse.'

'Come in and sit down,' she said tartly. 'I really would like to hear what you've got to say for yourself. I stayed up last night waiting for you to come like you promised. So why didn't you? You're the most unreliable man.'

'Give me something to eat, and I'll explain.'

She fetched him a loaf of bread, a big segment of cheese and a jug of beer which he proceeded to demolish rapidly.

'Now tell me,' she persisted. 'Why have you suddenly turned up here on Sunday night instead of Saturday, looking such a fright? What caused all those cuts on your arms?'

'Sugar, can I stay here for a few days to sort myself out? I'll give you a hand on the farm in payment. I'll work my passage. I'm not a scrounger.'

'All right. I suppose so. I couldn't turn a dog away in your condition. But why have you left Woodfield Hollow so suddenly? Here, Terry, have you been fighting again? I know you and your quarrelsome habits. And speaking of quarrelsome, do you know anything about my friend, Alvin Ballsover?'

'No,' he replied innocently. 'What's he done this time? Been in the wars with somebody else?'

'He's disappeared. That's what. Nobody's

seen him since Friday night.'

'So what?' said Terry casually. 'That's only two days. He's probably off on a bender, or humping some other well-stacked lady farmer in the district. He'll turn up, no sweat. Unpleasant buggers like him always do.'

'In that case why did he leave his Landrover in the car park at the Lord Burleigh on Friday night? Why did he arrange to go shooting over the estate on Saturday morning with Harry Pigott, the foreman at the Manor Farm? Alvin never turned up, and it's the first time he's ever missed an appointment in his life. Why would he just go off without a word to anybody?'

'I don't know. You know him better than I do,' replied Terry unconcernedly as he hacked himself off another great wedge of cheese.

'I was only thinking,' said Sugar, giving him a hard look, 'you came to blows with Alvin not long ago over me. You made all sorts of bloodcurdling threats against him, and I had to make you promise to lay off him.'

'So?'

'Well, it's not anything to do with you, is it, this disappearance? Some people seem to think Alvin's been done away with. He's just not the type to go off without a word to anybody.'

'Now look,' said Terry indignantly, 'what do you think I am, a bloody murderer? I admit I tangled with the ugly bugger once, but it was his doing, not mine. He attacked me. I've kept out of his way ever since. He's bigger than me. Besides, you know I wasn't anywhere near The Lord Burleigh on Friday night. I was here, covering you.'

'Yes, I know that. I'm sorry, Terry. But it's all very worrying. Alvin's been a good friend to me for a long time, and I'd be very grieved if something bad happened to him.'

'Like I said, I've not clapped eyes on him since he beat me up with a stick and smashed my bike up. Rough-housing with jealous idiots is not my scene.'

'So how did you come by all those cuts and scratches and looking so awful if you've not been brawling?' she persisted.

'And why do you want to stay here instead of with your friend at Woodfield Hollow?'

'That's just it. He's not my friend any more. We had a bust-up and he's another gorilla who's bigger than me and sadistic with it. So I had to run for it, like I did from Ballsover.'

'You must be a quarrelsome devil, Terry,' she said disapprovingly. 'You're always in the wars.'

'Well, it's not my fault. Just because I'm slightly built and look like a pushover every punch-happy, muscle-bound yokel thinks he can pick on me and knock me about.'

'But you've been living at his farm for months without trouble. You said he was your friend. Why would he suddenly want to knock you about?'

'Do you really want to know?'

'I asked you, didn't I?'

'You're not going to like it.'

'Tell me, Terry, for goodness sake!'

'Well, this bloke Haldane must have learnt to be AC/DC living out in the bush with the kaffirs, as he calls them.

197

I never dreamt he was like that. But last night he came home pissed and tried to bugger me. I got desperate to protect my virtue and punched him in the eye. Then he went berserk and came at me with a hunting knife. He really meant to carve me up. There was only one escape for me. I took a running dive at the window and crashed straight through, taking the whole bloody frame with me. Haldane came after me with his Doberman, and I've been biking round the countryside ever since to throw him off the scent. I made sure I'd lost him before I came here. I didn't want to involve you with a bugger like Haldane. He's real bad medicine.'

'Well, I must say, Terry, you have some very odd friends,' remarked Sugar, looking at him as with a new revelation. 'You obviously can't go back to Woodfield, so what happens to your rest in the country?'

'Could I stay here a week or two?'

'Oh, it's a week or two now, is it? It was only a few days at first.'

'The trouble is,' said Terry plaintively,

198

'I've left all my cash at Woodfield, diving through the window in such an emergency. If I try going back for it I could get my throat cut.'

'Why don't you tell the police all about Haldane and what he did to you?' exclaimed Sugar indignantly. 'He can't be allowed to attack people with knives and hunt them down with a Doberman. Does he think he's still in Rhodesia dealing with savages? You must go to the police, Terry.'

'Police!' echoed Terry with such a note of horror in his voice that Sugar gave him a look of frank bewilderment. 'No, not the police. They can't do anything for me, can they? I mean it's only my word against Haldane's, and he'll deny everything. It's never any good bringing the police into personal problems, because they don't want to know. I reckon I'll have to get back to the Smoke, London that is, and start up in my job again. First of all though I'll have to earn some money to buy my train ticket, so what about me working here for a spell?'

'All right,' she said. 'I suppose I can't

turn you away in the circumstances. But don't expect any fancy wage packets from me. I can only make a living on this farm by doing all the work myself.'

★ ★ ★

The presumption of foul play in Alvin Ballsover's sudden disappearance was so strong that the Regional Crime Squad with its headquarters in Northampton was called in to intensify the investigation. First of all they swooped on the old lodge-keeper's cottage at Aldingbourne Manor where Ballsover had lived, and gave it a thorough forensic examination. Routine analysis of the sparse contents of his medicine cabinet revealed that he had sufficient LSD tablets in the guise of aspirins to drive him to destruction many times over.

Most of the finger prints found on hard surfaces throughout the cottage were presumed to be Ballsover's, but there were also clear sets of alien finger prints on the aspirin bottle, the medicine cabinet and the window sill, which suggested that Ballsover had had a visitor in his bathroom planting LSD on him. The alien prints were lifted and sent to the central computer at Scotland Yard, which promptly revealed that Terence George Munton, escaped prisoner and drugs specialist, had somehow been involved with the missing man. This adequately explained the presence of a dangerous hallucinogenic drug in Ballsover's aspirin bottle. Also it made the suspicion of criminal action in Ballsover's disappearance a practical certainty. Allied to all this was the interesting deduction that Munton on the run had been operating in Northamptonshire, probably manufacturing LSD, and was still lying low there, on or near the Carvell estate.

All these significant developments were passed on to Detective Inspector Prosser of Criminal Intelligence at Scotland Yard, giving further pointers to a hazy and incredible surmise. For all this to be happening on the Carvell estate, and for Carvell's estate manager to be the suspected victim of criminal violence in association with Munton put a dark question mark over the minister's non-involvement, especially in view of his known affair with Elaine Cornford and the suspected criminal contacts of her husband Donald Carrington.

However, there was still insufficient evidence for a man of Digby Carvell's status to be treated as a suspect in a criminal conspiracy. Detective Inspector Prosser knew he had to wait patiently for even more significant developments before he could make a move.

15

By the time Terry Munton had lived on Vicar's Hill Farm for a week, working his passage, he realised that the earthy agricultural life was not for him. The peaceful, idyllic fulfilment he'd dreamed of down on the farm was all a myth. Sugar Fossett was a hard taskmaster, both in the bed and out of it. She had him up at the crack of dawn, helping her to milk the cows and feed the pigs. Then there were the broad beans and peas to be picked, the lettuces to be weeded, the carrots to be thinned. Before one job was finished there were several more lined up awaiting his attention. Sugar had never heard of trade union rules or the guaranteed eight-hour day. Her regime would have sparked off bloody riots in any prison. She kept him hard at it till the evening, and when he protested that he wasn't used to hard manual labour, she reminded him that there was nothing for nothing in this life. It had been his idea to earn his keep on the farm, and if he wasn't satisfied with the conditions of employment he could always get on his bike.

When it came to payday she was far from sugary in her generosity. She gave him ten quid for working a seven-day week anything up to twelve hours a day.

'What the bloody hell's this then?' he howled in incredulous dismay. 'You call this a man's living wage for all the hours I've put in?'

'It's as much as I pay myself,' she retorted, 'and it's only possible on a temporary basis unless I want a nasty little lecture from my bank manager. As for living, you've had your three square meals a day as well as the privilege of sharing a bed with the lady of the house. If you were a real gentleman you'd be paying me for your home comforts.'

'I am paying you over the odds with blood and sweat,' he fumed. 'It's slavery, exploitation, sucking my blood like a vampire.'

'So it is, Terry,' she retorted with a mocking smile. 'But you're not going to walk out on me, are you? You need to stay here far more than I need to have you here.'

'What do you mean?' he demanded in alarm.

'Oh yes, Terry, you do need me, don't you? And I'll tell you why. You know what I think, Terry? I think you're a bad lad and you're running away from somebody else as well as Haldane at Woodfield Hollow. I noticed in bed last night your hair isn't really black, is it? It's coming through a definite ginger at the roots. So I asked myself, why does he need to dye his hair and beard? Is it a disguise? And then I suddenly remembered how you nearly had kittens the other day when I mentioned you should go to the police about Haldane ill-treating you. You're on the run, aren't you, Terry? You really need a lonely little hide-out in the back of beyond.'

'You're not going to turn me in, are you?' he yelped in panic.

'Of course not,' she assured him

smoothly. 'We're very cosy together. I like having you as my own man about the house. You please me, even though you are a born idler and layabout and nowhere near as clever with your hands as poor Alvin used to be. I wouldn't want to lose you just yet, so I'm not going to hand you back to the police for whatever it is you've done. Someday perhaps the police may find out you're here and take you away, but it won't be my doing. Get on with your work now, Terry, there's a love. We farmers have to make the most of the daylight hours.'

So that was it! This crafty, mean-minded, big-boned country wench had sussed out his secret. Knowing he had nowhere else to hide, she was going to use it to keep him in her power. She wanted him as her personal body slave to hump her every night and flog his guts out in the fields all day, and all for a miserable ten quid a week. She was like the female Arachnid who killed and ate the male as soon as he'd serviced her. The Prisoners' Aid and Rehabilitation Society would love a clear-cut case like this to get their teeth into!

After brooding and seething with indignation over the injustice of it, Terry decided he wasn't going to stand for it. First of all he'd take a chance on returning to Woodfield Hollow to collect his money from its hiding place. He would be able to see from the road whether Haldane's car was there or not, and if Haldane was away it would be child's play to break into the farmhouse.

He watched his opportunity for several days until Sugar Fossett was working with the tractor, cutting the grass for silage on one of the outlaying fields. She owned a battered old Morris Minor estate car which she used for conveying her piglets to market and various other shopping trips to town. Alvin Ballsover was always doing minor repairs on it when he was around. She generally kept it in an old barn next to the house, and she left the ignition key in a pigeon-hole of her big, old-fashioned roll-top desk in the sitting room. Terry's sharp eyes had spotted that at a very early stage in their relationship.

At about four o'clock in the afternoon he left his appointed task of hoeing an onion field and slunk into the house to get the key. The old rust-bucket started with some difficulty shuddering and vibrating and giving off an unhealthy blue smoke as he drove it out of the farmyard into the lane. Then he was rattling round the country roads towards Woodfield Hollow seven miles away. He wondered whether Sugar would set the fuzz on him when she found out he'd nicked her car. Being a grasping peasant she probably would, but by that time he would be long gone and miles away.

He stopped the car among the trees on the hill that looked down into the hollow, but he could see no sign of Haldane's dark blue Datsun in its usual parking place. In fact the farm looked completely deserted with no sign even of Angus the Doberman. With a feeling of distinct unease Terry drove down into the farmyard and lined up the car for a fast getaway if necessary, leaving the engine running. He fully expected Angus to come bristling round the outbuildings to investigate the visitor, and hoped the hound would remember him as a friend. But there was nothing, not even a solitary hen scratching for food. Everything was suspiciously quiet.

In fact Haldane had bolted and gone into hiding as soon as he realised he'd failed to kill Terry. He knew it was only a matter of time before Munton was caught and told the police everything. A passer-by had noticed there was something wrong at Woodfield Hollow, with the abandoned Doberman going mad with hunger and eating all the hens. The RSPCA had been called in to deal with it, and had captured Angus by throwing a huge net over him before hoisting him into the back of a truck and taking him to kennels. The remaining livestock had been taken into care by Harry Pigott, the foreman at the Manor Farm, pending the reappearance of the tenant of Woodfield Hollow.

The kitchen window through which Terry had dived to safety more than a week ago was still a gaping hole, unrepaired and unveiled against the weather. He looked through it into the farmhouse kitchen and saw it still in the familiar state of untidy disarray it had always been in when he lived there with Haldane, but with a layer of wind-blown dust over everything. He went across to look at the prefabricated concrete shed where he'd worked for so long making the microdots. It was all locked up, and as the windows had always been fitted with opaque glass he couldn't tell whether the chemical manufacturing equipment was still there or not. It was all water under the bridge. He'd only come back to recover what was rightfully his, and he was sure by now that the whole farm was completely abandoned, as lifeless as if it had been visited by some killer plague.

He climbed through the kitchen window aperture and hurried upstairs to his former bedroom, having first armed himself with a stout-bladed kitchen knife to prise up the floorboard. His money was still there undisturbed between the joists, five-hundred pounds in cash and more than six thousand in credit divided among the pass books of several Building

Societies; the proceeds of working flat out for eight months in the profitable business of making LSD, until that bloodthirsty lunatic Haldane had ruined everything by trying to kill him.

Terry found that all the clothes he'd bought himself while living at the farm, five good suits, several casual jackets and trousers and innumerable pairs of trendy shoes were still in the wardrobe. He rolled them all up together and threw them in the back of the car. Then he drove away, still unseen and unchallenged, and breathed a deep sigh of relief when the drugs farm dropped out of sight behind him for the last time. Now all the uncertainty was behind him. It was to be a new life in London, with enough money behind him to make a fresh start and no more lousy criminals ruthlessly manipulating him for their own ends.

Soon he'd left the country lanes, had bypassed Kettering and was on the busy A509 heading south for Wellingborough. He thought he would keep on this road and join the M1 at Newport Pagnell.

This would take him right into London, assuming that the old heap hung together and stayed mechanically alive for long enough.

On the outskirts of Wellingborough a white police Rover of the Northants Constabulary was parked in a lay-by, its crew having a smoke and a natter as they watched the numerous cars and lorries hurtling past in the summer afternoon. Their eyes caught and held the battered, rusty old Morris as it rattled and bounced down the highway, piloted by a scruffy looking, nondescript character with unkempt hair and beard. They had nothing against scarecrows in clapped-out old bangers as such, provided they had the necessary tax, insurance and MOT qualifications. But when they saw that the scarecrow in question wasn't belted down in accordance with the law, it was a fair excuse for nicking him.

It was so long since Terry had driven a car in the normal law-abiding way that he was completely out of touch with the passing of the new law on seat belts. The arguments for and against Big Nanny saving feckless drivers from their own puerile folly had passed over his head without registering when the law came into force in the preceding January. So when he went off in Sugar Fossett's car it never entered his mind that he needed to wear a seat belt in order to make it legal.

The police car took off from the lay-by with its brash, aggressive, American-style siren blaring away, and Terry nearly died with fright when he saw it sitting squarely in his mirror right behind him with its blue roof-light flashing. There was no question of putting his foot down and leaving it behind. The big Rover pulled out alongside him and the hard-faced copper nearest to him made peremptory signals to him to pull in at the side of the road. Had they recognised him under his beard, he wondered despairingly, or had that bitch Sugar Fossett already reported her car as stolen?

The two coppers stopped close behind him, got out of their vehicle and sidled up to him with their usual nonchalant, gloating, cat-and-mouse approach to a law-breaker bang to rights.

'Good afternoon, sir,' said the senior wolly, who prided himself on his suave civility to the punters before nicking them. 'Were you aware that the law requires you to wear a seat belt when driving a motor vehicle?'

'What's that? Oh, I'm sorry, officer. I — I forgot,' gulped Terry, whose shifty nervousness was instantly noted.

'Is this your car, sir?'

'Yes, of course.'

'Would you mind telling me its registration number?'

Terry just stared at him in shocked dismay, wondering why he'd never even bothered to notice the number of Sugar's car before he drove off in it.

'Would you just mind stepping out of the car, sir?'

Terry did so, his knees turning to jelly.

'May I see your driving licence and certificate of insurance?'

'I — I don't carry them around with me,' he stammered. 'They're at home.'

'I see. And where would home be?'

'Vicar's Hill Farm,' said Terry with sudden inspiration. 'It's near Aldingbourne village.'

'Oh, you're the farmer, are you?' said the wolly sceptically.

'Well, no, not exactly.'

'A casual worker there perhaps?'

'Yes, that's right,' said Terry eagerly.

'What's your name?'

'Terence Murphy,' he replied promptly, thinking of the name on his Building Society pass books.

'And where are you heading for, Mr Murphy?'

'Just into town, into Wellingborough to get some shopping.'

'I'd have thought Kettering was a lot nearer to you for shopping than Wellingborough,' observed the wolly mildly.

'Well, er — '

'Do all these clothes and shoes belong to you, sir?' said the other constable who'd been mooching about inside the old car.

'Yes, of course they're mine.'

215

'Do you normally take your entire wardrobe with you when you go shopping?' said the policeman facetiously. 'Or don't you trust them with your clothes out at Vicar's Hill Farm?'

'I — I — '

'I'm not satisfied that you're the legal owner of this vehicle, sir,' said the first copper sternly. 'I shall have to detain you for further questioning until we've made enquiries as to the registration particulars of this vehicle.'

'Surely that's not necessary, officer,' blustered Terry desperately.

'Just get into the police car, sir. We'll lock up your car until someone can be sent out to take charge of it.'

As he obeyed, Terry could see already the grim, gnarled, gruesome gates of the Scrubs closing round him and the hustling into the Punishment Block, his precious freedom a dream of the past, and all the gone and wasted years, as they whisked him into Wellingborough Police Station. They stuck him in a bleak, demoralising interview room with a truculent and taciturn constable to guard him. While an enquiry was sent to the police computer operators at Hendon to find out who was the registered owner, of the old Morris, two policemen in a Panda car went out to Vicar's Hill Farm to check that the suspect really lived there as he claimed.

Sugar Fossett, having by this time missed her car and Terry, was fuming with indignation at his diabolical cheek in so taking her for granted as to walk off the job to go joy-riding in her car without even asking. She was going to give him a real roasting when he returned, and dock it out of his week's wages both for the time and the use of the car. She never dreamt he'd gone for good until the police arrived, asking her if she was the legal owner of the Morris Minor estate car which had been stopped heading south on the outskirts of Wellingborough, driven by a Terence Murphy who claimed to be resident at Vicar's Hill Farm.

When asked pointed and embarrassing questions about her whole relationship with Murphy and how she ever got involved with him, Sugar was so furious with him for bringing prurient, prying policemen into her home that she told them angrily all she knew about Terry and all she suspected: how he claimed to be a research chemist staying with a friend at Woodfield Hollow Farm; how he'd come crawling to her in a state of physical distress like a stray dog to be taken in when he'd been maltreated and menaced with a knife by Haldane the Rhodesian; how she knew he wasn't all he pretended to be because his hair was dyed black, growing out ginger at the roots. She even told them about Terry's confrontation with Alvin Ballsover, the bloodthirsty threats he'd made against Ballsover, and how the latter had mysteriously disappeared shortly afterwards. It looked as if he'd been done away with.

The policeman listened and wrote it all down in his little notebook with the usual painstaking thoroughness and deadpan lack of surprise. Then he asked her formally if she was prepared to swear in court that her car had been driven away without her consent.

'I certainly will!' retorted Sugar venomously. 'After all I've done for that bugger he robs me blind! I hope you lock him up and lose the key.'

16

By this time, having emptied Terry's pockets and found the five hundred pounds in cash plus the several Building Society accounts with credit for a further six thousand, the Wellingborough Police began to catch on that their random catch was no ordinary small-time villain who stole cars and went joy-riding for kicks.

When the report came back from Vicar's Hill Farm with all that Sugar Fossett had said about him, especially his black hair growing out ginger, they started to look at him with even greater interest. His interrogation was taken over by senior detectives. They sent his finger prints by telex to the national computer at Scotland Yard to find out if he was a regular customer. Before nightfall they knew that their routine check on a mere seat belt offender had netted them Terence George Munton known in the underworld as the Gingerman, manufacturer and dispenser of dangerous drugs, the great escaper from Wormwood Scrubs, who'd been at liberty for more than eight months.

★ ★ ★

To detective Inspector Prosser at C11, still groping patiently and apparently ineffectively towards the truth, it came as a startling surprise to hear that Munton had been captured in Northamptonshire, the county where the drugs trail had led and then petered out with the discovery of Charles Leplar's Volvo in a ditch.

Even more rewarding was that Munton had reneged on the creed of a whole lifetime and decided to make a deal with the Regional Crime Squad officers who were interrogating him. Faced with the threat of being put on trial for numerous drugs offences and for suspected foul play against the missing Alvin Ballsover, Munton realised he had no choice but to co-operate. In return for being allowed to finish his sentence at the Scrubs with no further charges and only a token loss of remission for escaping, he put the finger on Henry Haldane the Selous Scout, describing the whole operation of the drugs factory established at Woodfield Hollow, and how Haldane had admitted killing Ballsover because he'd snooped and become suspicious.

Munton also told of the death and burial of the unkown visitor to the farm in March, and led the detectives to the lonely grave in the woods where they found the decomposing body of Bradley Chawton. A team of detectives then swooped on Woodfield Hollow and discovered the chemical equipment still there intact just as Munton had described it, though Haldane when he cleared out had taken the last consignment of microdots with him.

At Scotland Yard there was nothing known about Henry Haldane except that he was a Rhodesian national, formerly an officer in the armed forces, who'd fled to Britain after independence because of his unpopularity with the new black régime in Zimbabwe. Somehow he'd obtained a Home Office permit as a permanent resident. Now however, after Munton's testimony, a warrant was issued for Haldane's immediate arrest, and his early capture was confidently expected.

★ ★ ★

'With the drugs factory on one of the Carvell farms, doesn't that implicate Golden Boy up to his neck in the conspiracy?' said Detective Sergeant Collins hopefully. 'Don't you think it's time we had a go at him and pricked his privileged complacency a bit? He must have been handing out resident permits like confetti to criminal aliens.'

'There's no hurry for Carvell,' said DI Prosser. 'He's not going anywhere. I'd prefer to wait till we've got our hands on that Selous Scout. By the way, the decomposed body that Munton led us to, buried in the woods a mile from the drug-makers' farm has definitely been established as Bradley Chawton. The FBI have confirmed it by his dental records, so his case is closed, thank

God. The locality of his death confirms our suspicion that he was part of the drug-making consortium. We assume he was killed at Woodfield Hollow over some criminals' quarrel, most probably by Haldane, which makes him absolutely vital to our case.'

'And what about the other bastard, Carrington?' said DS Collins.

'What about him?'

'Isn't there a strong presumption that he's been involved in all this? For my money he's the mastermind.'

'Maybe so,' said Prosser, 'but there's nothing we could use in the way of proof. In any case Carrington's disappeared. He's probably cleared off abroad for a spell now that his operation has been blown apart and the heat is on. Our big hope is to get our hands on Haldane and make some kind of deal with him to turn the others in. Without his evidence we've got next to nothing. Carrington has cleared up all his loose ends. Carvell too only needs to maintain total ignorance of what was going on at Woodfield Hollow. He can put all the blame on his estate manager for installing Haldane there as a tenant farmer, and Ballsover is nowhere around to contradict him. Let's not forget that Digby Carvell is first and foremost a politician. That means a lying, forked-tongued, double-thinking prevaricator with a genius for self-preservation. He'll have a fail-safe escape route from anything that could damage his golden future, unless, unless — '

'You mean unless one of the other charmers will turn Queen's Evidence out of spite or self-interest when he's really up against it and put the finger on Carvell?'

'Stranger things have happened,' nodded Prosser.

17

As far as Digby Carvell was concerned, the way things were developing in the great watershed of danger in his life, there was now some reason for a feeling of cautious optimism with the smashing of the drug-making syndicate. Of course Digby had been interviewed by the Regional Crime Squad officers from Northamptonshire about the disappearance of his estate manager. They questioned him closely on Ballsover's background, family and social connections, but of course Digby knew nothing to suggest the man had ever been involved with merchants of LSD or any other desperadoes. The very idea! He would never have employed Ballsover in any capacity if he'd had the least reason to doubt his integrity.

With the subsequent unmasking of the drugs factory at Woodfield Hollow, the same detectives had visited Digby again at his London flat, this time with a more brusque and stern approach as if they already had him in their sights as a possible suspect.

Was he aware of the serious implications of dangerous drugs being manufactured on his property?

Digby vehemently denied any knowledge of the criminal propensities of his tenant, firmly maintaining that he delegated all the running of the estate to his estate manager. It was Ballsover who'd brought in Haldane as a tenant farmer; Ballsover who must somehow have fallen into the hands of the criminals so that he danced to their tune. Perhaps his mysterious disappearance was all part of the same picture. Digby certainly didn't understand how he could be held responsible for the lawless activities of his appointed employee. However, he promised that in future he would personally supervise and vet all the tenant farmers who were allowed possessory rights to his property. Furthermore he would find time in the midst of his onerous State duties to make periodic inspections of his tenant farms to satisfy himself that nothing illegal was being done there.

The detectives went away far from satisfied, but reluctantly forced to concede that they would get no farther with Carvell. They resolved to have another hard drive on Munton to pressure him into admitting that he'd been involved with Carvell while he was working on drugs manufacture at the farm. But Munton had never even seen the estate owner. Henry Haldane was the only suspect he could give them with testimony to a double murder, but Haldane was nowhere to be found, and Digby began to hope he was as permanently lost as Ballsover.

Now that the drug-making conspiracy had finally been smashed Digby began to convince himself that Carrington could have no further demands to make on him. The little artificial scandal over Elaine now seemed very small beer when set alongside the wholesale distribution of drugs and the swift, ruthless removal of Ballsover as soon as he became a threat. Digby's knowledge of all that and his readiness to testify if pushed to it could be a countervailing weapon against any other squalid piece of blackmail that Carrington might try against him. It was a Mexican stand-off, and he was sure Carrington was shrewd enough to realise it.

★ ★ ★

Within two months of the end of the drugs factory Digby received a jolt more staggering than anything since the fateful day he'd gone down to Brighton to be confronted by Elaine's husband. As on the former occasion it came when he was least expecting it, when he was preoccupied with enjoyment at one of the prestigious London social functions that were the wine of life to him.

He was attending the *soirée* of a millionaire socialite in a large Georgian mansion backing on to the river at Kew. It was the kind of party where the host is like God, unseen and unapproachable but always displaying his wondrous works.

In the great reception rooms all the glittering quality of London Society seemed to have gathered in display, but suddenly it all turned as sour and abhorrent to Digby as if it had been just a lower middle-class hop in the village hall which he was attending to gratify his tenants. There, as large as life, talking animatedly to a tall, desiccated, vinegar-faced official from the French Embassy was Elaine Cornford, dressed in a magnificent green gown of billowing green tulle with a myriad tiny silver sequins sewn on by hand. She looked strikingly beautiful in her serenely restrained fashion, but Digby couldn't help shuddering at the lethal menace of what that beauty had already done for him.

She'd already spotted Digby before he could duck out of sight. She raised her finger and beckoned to him with a royal gesture as she made her hurried excuses to her French escort and homed in on her prey.

'Digby!' she gushed. 'But how delightful, how fortuitous to meet you here when

I've been absolutely aching to make contact.'

'I can't say the feeling is mutual,' he retorted with an ill-natured scowl. 'I'm barely out of the wood after that other ghastly mess you landed me in.'

'Really?' she said, her eyes wide with innocence. 'What mess was that? Oh Digby, how could you be so ungallant? But I'm determined to forgive you. If I hadn't found you here I was going to contact you at your ministry.'

'For God's sake, don't!' he snapped, angrily.

'But I must. The real reason why I wanted to see you was to pass on a message from Donald.'

'Oh no!' muttered Digby, his pulse quickening with alarm. 'Not that black-mailer again! Just tell him: I have nothing to say to him, and there's nothing I can do for him.'

'Oh Digby, but you must listen to what he has to say. He says it's absolutely vital, a matter of life and death for all of us. It's the last good turn he wants to do you for the sake of our old friendship.'

'Yes, my God! I know what his friendship is likely to land me in,' exclaimed Digby, close to desperation as he saw the old evil ascendancy threatening to engulf him again. 'All right then. I'll meet him just this once and hear him out. But you'd both better realise things have changed drastically since the last time I saw him. Your husband's lucky not to be in gaol already, and if he tries blackmailing me again he'll find it's not all one-sided. I know enough to put him well and truly behind bars.'

'Oh darling, you're so melodramatic. You're speaking dialogue from an old Reagan movie, and I'm afraid it's way above my head. Will you come with me now to meet Donald? He's at my house in Chelsea, patiently waiting.'

'For God's sake, not now!' he exclaimed pettishly. 'I'm attending a social function. Damn you and your husband. Let him wait.'

'I'm afraid he won't wait, darling. You should know Donald by now. He never waits. He'll be out of the country tomorrow, and the good turn he wants to do you will simply stay undone. It will be your loss, Digby. Your most grievous loss.'

Digby stared at her in exasperated rage, but then his lurking guilt, his fear of Carrington and his morbid curiosity to know what the villain was planning for him this time prompted his resigned acceptance. In fact he was almost eager to get it over and test the strength of his own counter-threat to Carrington.

Elaine went to get her mink stole from the cloakroom while Digby phoned for a taxi. A quarter of an hour later they were back in Elaine's house in Flood Street.

18

Donald Carrington was in the sitting room, ensconced in voluptuous comfort with his velvet smoking jacket, his big cigar and glass of bourbon and ice cubes. Though his profitable drugs manufacturing venture had been smashed, with Bradley Chawton mysteriously vanished without a word and Henry Haldane a hunted fugitive, Carrington had sailed serenly above the disaster with no viable evidence against him. He looked completely unruffled by events and still adopted the role of the spurious hearty towards his dupe.

'Hullo, old chap,' he beamed, advancing cordially to meet Digby with his hand outstretched. 'Still the golden boy, I hear, our bright political star. Congratulations on retaining your seat and your job.'

'What do you want this time?' said Digby tensely, looking at the black eyes and swarthy face with mingled resentment and revulsion. 'You horrify me.'

'Oh, really?' murmured Carrington unperturbed. 'Why is that then, Digby?'

'When I gave you a friendly warning about the suspicious of my estate manager, I'd no idea you were going to have him killed. As for setting up a drugs factory on one of my farms, your criminal audacity is beyond belief. How could you hope to get away with it?'

'Oh, come off it, Digby,' replied Carrington with a good-natured dismissive gesture. 'Who said I had your estate manager killed? I never laid a finger on him, or instructed anybody else to do so. I expect he'll be back to manage your estate again when he's finished his world cruise.'

'What! Do you mean that?'

'Elaine, darling,' said Carrington, 'why don't you go back to the ball and enjoy yourself? Digby and I have man's talk to do, some boring logistical problems to mull over. You'd find it very tiresome.'

'Oh, very well then, darling,' said Elaine with her bright smile. 'If you're sure you can manage without me I'll gladly go back and enjoy myself. Back in the small hours, darling. Goodnight Digby.'

As the outer door slammed behind her, Carrington poured the drinks and motioned to Digby to sit down in one of the armchairs at the fireside.

'So what's this talk about a marvellous good turn you're going to do me?' queried Digby. 'Was it just a ploy to get me here, and how much is it going to cost me?'

'We share a common trouble and a common threat, you and I,' said Carrington bluntly. 'In a word, Henry Haldane the Rhodesian soldier of fortune.'

'Haldane? I've never met the man, even though he took the tenancy of one of my farms. It was you who appointed him to manage your disreputable drugs factory, and the police know all about him now. I don't see how he concerns me.'

'Digby,' said Carrington sadly, 'you're either very naive or you're being deliberately obtuse. Aren't you forgetting it was you who wangled him his Home Office permit to live here as a resident alien? It would never do for that good turn to become public knowledge when Haldane is in the dock. Apart from that, Haldane knows all about your supportive role in siting the drugs factory on one of your farms, just as he knows enough about me to put me up the steps at the Old Bailey. That's why he came to me to do something for him after the débâcle up at the drugs factory when he had to go into hiding pretty fast. If the police get their hands on him now he could make a deal in the hope of getting a lighter sentence. He could give them you and me.'

'My God!' muttered Digby, ashen-faced with terror. 'You mean you're hiding him?'

'In a manner of speaking. Not in this house, of course. Various places up and down the country. I've found him a flat in London, a country cottage, a rented caravan at a seaside resort, rooms at various hotels and boarding houses, anything to keep him on the move round the country. Staying too long in one place may spark off some nosey bugger's curiosity. But it's getting too big a problem for me to handle on my own. You've got to help now, Digby. You're in this up to the neck. It's just as much in your interest as mine that we keep that bloody-minded Rhodesian bastard out of the hands of the police.'

'But what do you expect me to do about it?' cried Digby despairingly. 'You know as well as I do you can't keep a man on the run indefinitely in this country. It's only a matter of time before the police get their hands on him.'

'I know,' said Carrington morosely. 'A real honey of a problem, isn't it? Ideally we should get him out of the country to some place like South Africa where he'll feel at home, with enough money to set him up there so that he'll stay put and trouble us no further. That's why I'm relying on you for help, Digby. I know you find raising money is no problem.'

'I see. I knew it was all coming back to money,' said Digby sourly. 'How much money?'

'If you can put up half of what's needed, say two hundred grand — '

'What! Two hundred thousand pounds! That's ridiculous.'

'Oh, is it?' countered Carrington sharply. 'Well, just consider the alternative and you'll realise it's dirt cheap to a man in your position. Like it or not, Digby, we've got a door to shut, and if we don't shut it properly we're both down the river. We're allies now, fending off a common mortal danger. It's not a question of me trying to screw you or take advantage of your position any more.'

'Christ!' blasphemed Digby, his spirits in deep eclipse. 'You must be mad to think you could set up some squalid drugs factory in this country and make a fortune without getting caught. And why did you have to drag me down with you?'

'Well, you know me, Digby,' replied Carrington, smugly unrepentant. 'The eternal entrepreneur, that's me. I look around for a sizeable hole in the market and then get tooled-up to fill it, at a reasonable working profit of course. And as for dragging you down, old boy, it was you if you remember who first dragged yourself down into my world by your honcho bedroom athletics, humping women you can't afford. Anyway, all that how and why business is completely irrelevant. It's the burning practical emergency we've got to deal with now. Are you prepared to put up the money to get Haldane out of the country and guarantee our future safety? Or are you going to be the richest, best behaved, most highly born prisoner in Wormwood Scrubs?'

'Supposing I do supply that amount of money,' said Digby in pettish despair. 'How can I be sure it's a once-for-all payment? What guarantee is there that when he's spent or lost his money in South Africa, Haldane won't come back here, demanding to be bought off again with some even bigger extortionate sum of money?'

'Of course there's no guarantee. What control can I possibly have over Haldane's future activities when he's gone abroad?'

'Well, I would have thought that somebody with your criminal talents and ingenuity could arrange a final solution to the problem for a fraction of what it's going to cost to maintain Haldane for the rest of his life as an emigré playboy,' said Digby savagely.

For a moment Carrington seemed stunned. Then he gave a peal of mocking laughter.

'Well done, Digby old boy,' he applauded. 'I always knew you had it in you. You really are in my world, for all your Golden Boy, born-to-the-purple gentility and education. Correct me if I've got you wrong. You're suggesting that we put up money to hire a technician to liquidate Haldane the sooner the better. Right?'

'Right,' said Digby unbashed. 'He's only a criminal of the most degraded and despicable kind, no loss to anybody as far as I can see, but with the power and will to cause an awful lot of misery. It would be an investment in common decency as well as ensuring our own safety from him.'

'Just as a matter of interest,' chuckled Carrington with genuine amusement, 'when there's a free vote in the House of Commons about bringing back the Death Penalty, on which side do you cast your vote?'

'I don't see how that's at all relevant to this case,' snapped Digby. 'But since you ask, I'm all for abolition. Judicial murder by the State is a relic of barbarism that shames every civilised country. We in Parliament have to be in advance of brutish public opinion, not slavishly following it.'

'Ask a silly question!' said Carrington, still chuckling to himself. 'Oh boy! What a loss and what a tragic waste if you should ever be lost to politics! So you'd really feel safer and a good deal better if Haldane had the final solution applied?'

'Certainly. Wouldn't you?'

'You're just a bloodthirsty amateur. You don't even begin to understand the nature of the problem,' said Carrington contemptuously. 'In the States of course there's no difficulty about termination. You just find your hit-man in the Yellow Pages under Technical Services. You put down your ten thousand dollars with the name and address of the mark. Within a week he's cleanly and anonymously terminated with no repercussions, no blackmail and no embarrassing police enquiries coming home to your door. Your hit-man there is a true professional. But in this country, if you hire a contract killer the best that can happen is that he'll bungle it. If he's successful he'll be coming to you with blackmail demands for the rest of his stinking life. The worst and most likely thing to happen when you go shopping for a killer is that the fuzz will have been tipped off somewhere along the way. So when you hand over the blood money to your so-called hit-man, he promptly snaps a bracelet on your wrist and announces himself as Detective Constable Gormless, who wants you to help him with his enquiries. In this benighted country, if you want a man killed the only safe guaranteed way is to do it yourself with all the risks. There's no professional integrity here.

'So if Haldane is to be clinically removed from our hair, it's either got to be you or me or both of us acting together. How's your bottle then, Digby? If I set Haldane up for you in a convenient meeting place and get you a weapon, are you prepared to kill him with your own hands?'

'I — I — No, of course not,' muttered Digby breaking out into a sweat.

'That's what I thought. You're just so much soft pap under that Golden Boy, House of Commons glitter of the ruling élite. It so happens that I'm no butcher either. I'm prepared to bend the law every other way, but when it comes down to murder I know my limitations. It would be courting disaster even to try. So that leaves us back where we started: to arrange a safe passage out of the country for Haldane, and make it worth his while never to come back. Are you with me?'

'I — I suppose so,' muttered Digby in sick despair.

'Good,' beamed Carrington with jovial cordiality. 'Let's get down to the nitty-gritty then. I'll take care of all the negotiations with Haldane and fix up the private plane that'll ferry him across the Channel from an airstrip in Kent. All you have to do is put up your share of the money, two hundred grand. I'd like it in a banker's draft made payable to me in person.'

'But look here,' protested Digby, suddenly taking fright at the awesome prospect of parting with so much money in such a dubious cause as an act of pure faith to a known criminal. 'How do I know you're being square with me? How do I know there's any threat from Haldane at all, or even that he's still in the country? How do I know that all this charade you're putting on to frighten me is not just one of your entrepreneurial tricks to swindle me out of two hundred thousand?'

'You don't know I'm not screwing you,' said Carrington calmly. 'In this situation you can't possibly know. There's no way I can give you proof here and now that Haldane is on the run, prepared to make a deal with the fuzz if he gets caught. But if you won't go along with me and Haldane is left running loose in this country, you'll bloody soon find out how badly you're getting screwed — in the slammer. You can take it or leave it, Digby. If you won't co-operate with me to clear up this mess, I'll be on a flight to South America in the morning, and you can have the hypothetical Haldane all to yourself.'

'All right,' gulped Digby brokenly. 'I can see I have no choice. But to raise such a sum I shall have to dispose of certain assets. Nobody keeps that amount of money uninvested. It'll take about a week.'

'Well, all right,' frowned Carrington. 'A week will have to do, but I don't feel easy about it. It's extending the danger period. Any day now Haldane could run out of luck and be in the hands of the fuzz. I'll keep my fingers crossed, and my reservation to South America constantly renewed.'

19

Four days later Digby received a peremptory telephone call from Carrington demanding another urgent meeting at the house in Chelsea, an invitation which Digby was in no position to refuse. Carrington sounded rattled if not actually panicky, a development which Digby knew with foreboding could only mean more bad news for himself.

'Have you raised the money yet?' demanded Carrington as soon as Digby was over the threshold.

'Not quite. Two more days for the final assets to be realised. You gave me a week, remember.'

'I know,' muttered Carrington tight-lipped. 'I was being unduly optimistic.'

'Why? What's happened?'

'Bloody Haldane is becoming paranoid is what's happened. He's broken off contact. You can't call me, he says. I'll call you.'

'Why?'

'He thinks I'm stalling with the money while I set things up to have him killed.'

'And you're not of course,' said Digby hopefully.

'Oh, for Christ's sake, we've been through all that and decided it's not on. No doubt it's what Haldane himself would do if our roles were reversed. But I've told you why contract killing is too risky for me to have anything to do with in this country. I'd just found him a safe little furnished flat in East Finchley, but he reckons he was a sitting duck for my hit-man there. So he's moved out into the centre of town and rings me up to give me instructions.'

'What instructions?'

'The only place he'll agree to meet me to collect the going-away money and the new passport is in your Park Lane flat.'

'Good God!' exclaimed Digby in dismay. 'Why there?'

'Because of your high respectability he thinks your flat is the only place where we wouldn't dare to have him killed. It would be fouling your own doorstep, and you have too much to lose. It would be as fatal to you as letting Haldane do his worst in the police station.'

'Of course he's right,' said Digby shrill with alarm. 'It would be virtually impossible to move a body out of that building without somebody spotting it. There's an ex-Marine hall porter on duty in the vestibule twenty-four hours a day for security reasons.'

'I know that, and so does Haldane. He's going to call the meeting at short notice sometime in the late evening, any day next week or the week after, to keep us off-balance so that we can't lay on a set-piece ambush outside the building. He's a Selous Scout still fighting his war in the bush. So you'd better make your social engagements fairly undemanding, like staying at home every night with pressure of work until Haldane has been and gone.'

'Who does that arrogant swine think he is?' fumed Digby. 'Presuming to dictate a total freeze on my private life!'

Carrington laughed unpleasantly.

'Of course we all know your priorities are with your dong,' he scoffed. 'I can think of an even more permanent freeze on your private life if Haldane doesn't get away free and clear. The successful exporting of Haldane had better take precedence even over your tom-catting for the next fortnight. And by the way, Digby, do you keep a car in London to help your private enterprise?'

'Yes, I have a car here.'

'Where do you keep it?'

'In the basement garage underneath the Park Lane flats. Why?

'It's a pretty anonymous, run-of-the-mill sort of vehicle for your purposes, I presume?'

'It's a Mitsubishi Colt.'

'What else but Jap crap!' sneered Carrington sourly. 'Trust you trend-setters in Government to do your bit for the poor old British car worker. Have you got the car here?'

'No, I came by taxi. It was easier this time of day.'

'Do you keep the car locked when it's in the garage?'

'Yes, I always try to remember it.'

'Do you have a spare key?'

'Yes, I think so. What for?'

'Give it to me.'

'But I don't carry it about with me. It's at my flat.'

'Get it to me here, as soon as possible, like today.'

'What on earth for?' protested Digby.

'It occurs to me that Haldane, the Rhodesian counter-terrorist, knows a trick or two about spiking cars. I wouldn't want him booby-trapping yours out of spite once he's got his money.'

Digby stared at him in shocked disbelief. 'But this is sheer melodramatic nonsense,' he exclaimed. 'I've never even met Haldane, so why should he have it in for me after I've put up the money to give him a new life abroad?'

'Listen, Digby old boy, you just stick to your committee back-scratching and political fixing and fat-cat self-indulgence. I know that bugger Haldane from way back, and how his twisted mind works. He was in the Selous Scouts, the most efficient bloodthirsty bastards in Africa, and the worst shits. Note the mob's initials: SS. He feels really lost without the howls of niggers dying in the bush. Although you may be shocked to hear it, he loathes you Bertie Woosters in the British Government even more than he loathes the bloody Reds. He blames you for betraying your own white tribe in Africa, selling out your kith and kin to black commie savages with your sanctimonious, nigger-loving trendiness. He reckons you get a hard-on every time you think about niggers. He'd cheerfully murder the bloody lot of you in both Houses of Parliament if he could. So don't argue. Give me your spare car key, and I'll run a check on your Jap crap after Haldane has been paid off and gone, just to make sure it won't blow your arse off when you turn the ignition key.'

'I'll deliver the key to you later on today without fail,' promised Digby earnestly. 'But why are you doing this for me? I'd have to be very naive not to wonder about your ulterior motive.'

'Absolutely no ulterior motive, Digby old boy,' said Carrington with a genial wink. 'I told you, you're part of the family since you made such an impression on Elaine. It would be extremely short-sighted of me, as well as damned ungrateful, not to keep you alive and functioning in government for as long as possible. I mean, you're a big, juicy tit to squeeze and I just hate to let you go. As a matter of fact at the moment there's an Italian friend of mine, Mario Gabiani, an international business-man and entrepreneur, who's under a bit of a cloud at present with European governments and various pricks of that ilk. He badly needs the cachet of top-drawer respectability to be in line again for the best government contracts. So I reckon if you and the Lady Lucinda were to be photographed by the *paparazzi* with Gabiani and his wife and me and Elaine at his villa on the Algarve — a distinguished little family party — it would go a long way towards rehabilitating Gabiani among the social climbers with their hands on the levers of power. Anyway, we'll talk about it at a more congenial time when Haldane has finally vanished into the wide blue yonder.'

20

Eight days later at eleven o'clock at night Digby was alone in his flat, restlessly listening to some Bach on the stereo, and trying to occupy himself with some dry-as-dust ministerial papers, when he should have been out at some glittering *soirée*, lining up new talent, if it hadn't been for the threat hanging over him from that swine Haldane.

The telephone on his desk suddenly gave a discreet warble and Carrington's voice came on the line.

'Digby? It's on tonight. Our man is on his way over to your place. I'll get there as soon as I can. If he arrives first, just let him in, make him at home and tell him I'm on my way with the goods.'

'Yes, but look here,' gulped Digby in a sudden panic, 'I don't feel safe alone here with a man like Haldane. I mean, given that your account of his political and racist fanaticism is true — '

'He won't do anything to you,' said Carrington reassuringly. 'At any rate not until he's got his money and his new passport from me. Just hang in there, Digby. Be your usual charming self, until I get there to hold your hand.'

Less than five minutes afterwards the intercom buzzer sounded in the hall, the signal from the hall porter that he had a visitor. Digby picked up the handset of the wall telephone and announced himself.

'Mr Carvell, sir,' said the hall porter deferentially. 'A gentleman here to see you. He says it's by appointment. A Mr Ian Smith.'

'Very well. Yes, I'm expecting him. Send him on up,' said Digby in the crisp authoritative, slightly blustering tone he used in the House of Commons when covering up for the inept old buffer who stubbornly refused to fall under a bus.

Two minutes later the doorbell rang and Digby, his heart thumping with dread and sweat breaking out all over him, opened up to the Selous Scout.

Haldane while on the run had been

going about in various disguises with the help of a few theatrical props he'd acquired. At present he was dressed up like a top civil servant or bank manager in a blue serge suit, neat form-fitting charcoal grey overcoat and black homburg. He wore heavy black-rimmed glasses and a neat tooth-brush moustache which blurred but did not completely obscure the harsh identity of Henry Haldane. He looked at the svelte, handsome minister with ill-concealed contempt in his cold pale eyes.

Dressed in casual slacks and deep mauve velvet smoking jacket with a silk cravat knotted loosely at his throat, and his wavy quiff nodding forward over his handsome brow, Digby looked the archetypal closet hero who'd left his shoes under the most distinguished beds in London.

'So you're Golden Boy, then?' said the Rhodesian as he stepped inside. 'One of Her Majesty's best, eh? Good of you to give me an audience. Is Carrington here yet?'

'No, but he told me he's on his way.'

'With the necessary loot, I trust?'

'There wouldn't be much point in meeting you here otherwise,' observed Digby.

'That's right, Digger. Just as well you two beauts understand what's going to happen if the money's not all there or there's any smell of a doublecross.'

'I can assure you there's going to be nothing like that,' Digby hastened to assure him. 'In view of the ghastly mess you've got us all into with your wretched drugs factory, you can't leave the country soon enough or go far enough away for me.'

Haldane appraised him with a contemptuous grin.

'You bloody politicos are all the same whatever you're into,' he sneered. 'Bent, wet and windy, and always ready to hang a bribe on a feller, eh, Digger?'

'May I get you a drink?' said Digby with diplomatic servility, crossing the room to his well-loaded drinks trolley.

'Nothing for me,' said Haldane with his mirthless grin. 'I know it wouldn't really be worth your while to have me drop dead in here. But I don't take chances all the same. With the wonders of modern technology you might slip me something with a delayed action that wouldn't start to work for three hours, and then crease me up when I was long-gone from here.'

'My goodness me, what appalling company you must keep,' shrugged Digby at his most superior.

'Sure, feller, and you're the top of the flaming heap.'

Digby sat down uneasily in an armchair and sipped at his vodka and tonic, while Haldane wandered restlessly round the sumptuous room, examining the eighteenth century sporting prints that adorned the walls and the costly silver cups and porcelain figurines that Digby needed to have around him.

After about twenty minutes the hall porter sounded the intercom buzzer again and announced the arrival of another visitor, Mr Donald Carrington. The latter, dressed in dinner jacket, white silk scarf and black overcoat, and carrying a large briefcase, pushed into the flat past

Digby as if he wasn't there, and fixed cold, hostile eyes on the Rhodesian.

'So you're out from under your stone at last, Haldane, you awkward bugger,' he began disagreeably. 'You'd have saved yourself a hell of a lot of trouble and me lot of aggravation if you'd stayed put in the flat I found for you.'

'Yeah, Carrington, and I could also be dead by now,' retorted Haldane bluntly. 'I've been around long enough to know when I'm about to be had by the bloody rats. I've got a nose for rats. But if you've done your part like we agreed, I'll be out of your hair for good by tomorrow. So let's see the colour of what you've got in there.'

Carrington laid the briefcase on a chair and pressed the catches to open it up.

'Two hundred thousand pounds, as agreed. Three hundred thousand U.S. dollars. Half in U.S. hundred-dollar bills and half in U.S. Treasury bearer bonds.'

Haldane picked up the bundles of currency notes and examined them carefully one by one to make sure it wasn't filled out in the middle with blank paper. Then he picked up each bearer bond certificate and scrutinised it carefully, holding it up to the light.

'OK, they'll do,' he said at length. 'And now the rest of it, my new identity and my ticket out of this bloody shambolic island.'

Carrington took an envelope from his breast pocket.

'Here's your passport with your new identity, and here's the address of the man in Lydd with the private aircraft. His name is Blunt. He's a crop sprayer flying over in the morning to negotiate a deal with some French farmers at Abbeville. He's filed his usual flight plan for the airfield there. He's been paid and is expecting you. You'll find it a tight squeeze in the cabin of a crop sprayer, but you wouldn't expect to be going first-class. Officially you'll be his private secretary. So as soon as you're down on French soil you'll be able to melt away, hire yourself a car and disappear into the sunset, and bloody good riddance. I wouldn't think you'd be daft enough to come back here this side of the twenty-first century.'

'Too bloody right,' grinned Haldane. 'Not that it wouldn't be worth it to see the bilious look on the faces of you two buggers who think you've got it made.'

'By the way,' said Carrington in a reasonable tone, 'if it'll help you on your way I've got a Hertz hire car that I came in down in the basement garage. I'll drive you down to Lydd and deliver you right to the house of this guy Blunt. It'll save you time searching for his place.'

Haldane's wolf-like grin widened into a great guffaw.

'Can't get rid of me fast enough, eh Carrington?' he jeered. 'You two solid citizens will be shitting yourselves with fright until I'm safe over the water. Thanks a million, but no thanks. With you as my chauffeur, Carrington, and one of your underworld rats as back-up, I wouldn't like to think of all the things that could happen in that bloody car between here and Lydd.'

'Suit yourself,' said Carrington, swallowing his annoyance with an obvious effort. 'You'll soon be too bloody paranoid to step outside the door.'

'Considering what a total shit you are, Carrington, that's hardly surprising. Come to think of it though, maybe it wouldn't be a bad idea if I did take your Hertz car. I've got to get to Lydd somehow tonight, and taxi drivers are all clever buggers who remember faces and talk to the fuzz. Hand over the keys then.'

'Certainly,' said Carrington, proffering the car key with such alacrity that Haldane stared at him with quickening suspicion.

'On second thoughts, though,' said Haldane, 'if Hertz have to go to Lydd to collect their abandoned car, they'll report it to the fuzz who might pick up a trail at Lydd and tip off the French about an illegal immigrant coming in on a flight plan from Lydd. Then that bugger Blunt will spill the beans if they put the screw on him.'

'My God! You are in a permanent state of terror for a big bad Selous Scout,' sneered Carrington. 'Are you sure you've got the bottle to risk leaving London at all?'

'I've got a better idea than the Hertz car,' said Haldane, ignoring him. 'Hey, Digger, do you keep a car here?'

'Yes, of course,' said Digby with a startled look.

'Good. I'll take that then to get me down to Lydd. I'm bloody sure old Digger here won't want to tell the fuzz I've got his car. He'll go quietly down to Lydd and pick up his car in his own time without mentioning to anybody that I borrowed it to speed me on my way. Isn't that so, Digger?'

'You know I have no choice but to do everything in my power to keep you out of the hands of the police,' replied Digby tight-lipped.

'Right!' snapped Haldane. 'Consider your car commandeered in a good cause. Where do you keep it?'

'In the basement garage underneath here.'

'Description and number, and let's have the key.'

Digby gave him the particulars of his car and handed over the ignition key.

'OK then,' said Haldane with a triumphant grin as he closed up the briefcase and headed for the door. 'I'm on my way. I won't say thanks for the memory, because it's been all too typical of this lousy country and the crooks who run it. If we ever do meet up again it'll only be because everything's come unglued and we're all in the slammer together.'

As the outer door closed vigorously behind him, the tension in the room seemed to collapse like a pricked balloon.

With a look of sheer elation on his face Carrington sank into a nearby chair and broke into great peals of laughter, slapping his knee and wiping his eyes with childish delight.

'He bought it!' he gasped breathlessly. 'I outguessed the cunning bastard! That bloody clever survivalist the Selous Scout, he walked right into it.'

'Into what? What are you talking about?

What's so funny?' demanded Digby, regarding Carrington in his fatuous mirth with distaste and resentment.

'That bloody Rhodesian is going on a far longer journey than he thinks,' guffawed Carrington malevolently. 'Give him three minutes to be on his way. Then we'll go down to the garage and tidy him away.'

'What? You mean you've booby-trapped my car?' gasped Digby, pale with horror and revulsion.

'Not so that you'd notice,' chuckled Carrington. 'Nothing so coarse or common or unsophisticated as a bomb that breaks windows and starts fires and brings all the fuzz in Scotland Yard down on your head. I'm no common street hoodlum, Digby.'

'Then what have you done to my car?' persisted Digby tensely.

'Three minutes, I said. Then you'll see. You didn't really think I was going to let the swine walk out of here with two hundred grand, and still have power to send me to the slammer some day?'

★ ★ ★

In an unhurried and dignified fashion as befitted his dress and image, Haldane walked down the thickly-carpeted staircase to the entrance hall, at the back of which was a self-closing mahogany door with an illuminated neon sign above it that said: GARAGE.

Haldane went through it and down a flight of concrete steps to the large basement garage. Here the owners' cars were neatly lined up in bays between the square steel supporting pillars of the building, and the whole area was adequately illuminated by a system of strip lighting. At this hour the whole place was deserted. The squares were in bed, and the thrusters were still out on the town.

Haldane walked between the rows of silent cars till he spotted a Mitsubishi Colt Galant, and verified its ownership by checking with the registration number that Digby had given him. He inserted the key in the doorlock on the driver's side and flung open the door. Immediately a small pink capsule affixed to the top inside of the door-frame and activated by the door's opening squirted a five-second long burst of lethal gas into his face. It was a nerve gas so powerful that the slightest inhalation or even its touch on the skin could be fatal.

Haldane staggered back choking in agony, his hands clutching desperately at his chest as the vaporised poison paralysed his arteries and brought on all the symptoms of a massive coronary heart attack. With his face hideously contorted to a grotesque caricature of its living likeness he collapsed on the concrete floor, jerking and convulsing until he lost consciousness and was dead in a few seconds.

Carrington and Carvell arrived in the garage and walked quickly between the rows of cars to the scene of death. Carrington stepped over the prostrate body and with his gloved hand quickly detached the spent capsule from the door-frame, wrapped it in a handkerchief and dropped it in his pocket.

'It's known in the trade as a Pink

Panther,' he chuckled conversationally. 'CIA operatives use them all the time for removing foreign politicians hostile to U.S. interests, particularly in Central and South America. I brought a couple back with me from the States in case of an emergency like this. I used to work with an ex-CIA man who'd come over to the other side. Contacts are everything, no matter what you're into. You as a politician wouldn't give me any argument about that.'

Digby just stared at him, morally shattered into speechlessness as he recognised the evil ascendancy over him that would only end with his life. He felt physically nauseous with the realisation of how easily the contorted body at his feet could have been his own.

'How did you know he was going to take my car when you planted that thing there?' gasped Digby.

'I didn't know,' replied Carrington calmly. 'It was an intelligent guess based on my knowledge of Haldane.'

'Then — then you were gambling with my life. You didn't give a damn whether it was I or Haldane who opened that car door.'

'Well, you can't live without some risk,' said Carrington cheerfully. 'It's often unsafe to be alive in this world. But I really did hope it would be Haldane who bought the farm for obvious reasons. Besides, you can be such a gem with your seals of office! Come on then, Digby. Snap out of it. Help me into the car with him. Or do you want Haldane with his load of guilt found dead on your doorstep alongside your car?'

Heaving and panting they managed to haul the large inert body of Haldane into the back of Digby's car, pushing him down on the floor between the seats so that he wasn't easily visible.

'That's the ticket,' said Carrington breezily, slamming the car door on the stiff. 'A happy issue out of all our afflictions, as they say in church! Now you can return to normal living, Digby. Get on the blower to some little playmate, and erase the name Haldane from your consciousness. I'll go and lose him somewhere out of the environment, and then deliver your car back here.'

'You mean you don't need my help?'

'No. Haldane is my responsibility. I alone shall know where the body is, and that's a kind of insurance in itself.'

He started up the car, switched on the headlights and drove out towards the ramp that led upward into Park Lane. Digby was still so shattered by the horrible events that he didn't realise until the car had disappeared that Carrington had gone off with the briefcase containing two hundred thousand pounds that Haldane no longer needed. On Haldane's decease it had automatically become Carrington's.

21

In the mansion block there lived a retired Civil Service mandarin, Mr Dudley Osborne, OBE. He was one of the Left-inclined movers and shakers of the British Establishment who manipulate ministers for their own good and shape long-term national policy and preside languorously over genteel decay, while governments come and go, huffing and puffing during their brief lifetimes about shifting the huge inertia of the Civil Service.

On his huge inflation-proof pension and the money amassed over the years from his princely salary, Dudley Osborne lived comfortably in the flat adjoining Digby's. He was deeply interested in all aspects of the life of the rising young minister, and tried to retain some vestige of his own days of glory by closely observing the activities of Golden Boy. In fact Dudley Osborne's only obsession in life — if so staid and old-maidish a character could have an obsession — was to monitor Digby's comings and goings, to take note of the political colleagues, the social lions and the various women who beat a trial to Digby making things hum in the new modern way which Dudley Osborne, alas! had never known. He knew Digby's silver grey Colt Galant very well for he parked his own car alongside it in the basement garage.

That night when he was returning home from his pre-bedtime stroll in Hyde Park and turning into Park Lane by Grosvenor Gate, he suddenly spotted and recognised Digby's car cruising down the road in the sparse night-time traffic towards him. He verified by the registration number that it was certainly Digby's car. He knew the minister had been at home in his flat all evening for he could see the light streaming out on to the balcony adjoining his own. It was distinctly odd for Digby to be going off somewhere at this hour.

As the car drew abreast of him Dudley Osborne directed a sharp enquiring look at the man behind the wheel, clearly illuminated by the street lighting, and realised with a shock of outrage that somebody else had taken the minister's car. It was a total stranger, a dark swarthy man who certainly looked enough of a cad to steal a fellow's car.

Dudley Osborne didn't believe in leaving anything to chance or giving anybody the benefit of the doubt when he witnessed what he thought to be a blatant felony. The police did little enough to keep crime off the streets or out of the home, and the irrecoverable thefts of cars in London had reached pandemic proportions. Dudley Osborne had no doubt he would be doing his neighbour the minister an inestimable service by reporting and thus frustrating the theft of his car.

He hurried into the mansion block, asked the hall porter for the use of his phone, and put through a call to West End central Police Station. He informed the officer on duty that he was reporting the theft of a car from the basement garage in Hamilton Towers, Park Lane. He'd just seen the thief drive it away, heading north along Park Lane towards Marble Arch. He gave the make, description and registration number of the vehicle, and insisted that if the police acted promptly they would catch the car thief *in flagrante delicto*, in possession of his booty on the highway.

Thus it happened that as Carrington drove sedately west down Bayswater Road on his own private funeral procession, heading for the Great West Road and the open country beyond, his blood suddenly congealed with horror when he heard the strident wail of a police siren right on his tail. A lurking police car, having received the radio message about a probable stolen car approaching their area, spotted the registration number on the Galant and came swooping out of a side-road to overtake. The police car forced Carrington into the side of the road, and two police constables converged on him.

In a state of abject terror, his face having taken on a dirty grey pallor, Carrington could do nothing but cower behind the steering wheel as he waited for the sky to fall in on him. There were no contingency plans against this emergency. He felt as if he was attending his own funeral. Now he knew how things inexorably must end.

The policemen asked him briefly if the car was his and if he had any documentation to prove it. Then they abruptly forgot all about a mundane peccadillo like car-stealing when they had a quick routine look inside the car and spotted the contorted body of Haldane lying hunched up on the floor between the front seat and the back.

'Do you know anything about this body, sir?'

THE END

A LANCE FOR THE DEVIL
Robert Charles

The funeral service of Pope Paul VI was to be held in the great plaza before St. Peter's Cathedral in Rome, and was to be the scene of the most monstrous mass assassination of political leaders the world had ever known. Only Counter-Terror could prevent it.

IN THAT RICH EARTH
Alan Sewart

How long does it take for a human body to decay until only the bones remain? When Detective Sergeant Harry Chamberlane received news of a body, he raised exactly that question. But whose was the body? Who was to blame for the death and in what circumstances?

MURDER AS USUAL
Hugh Pentecost

A psychotic girl shot and killed Mac Crenshaw, who had come to the New England town with the advance party for Senator Farraday. Private detective David Cotter agreed that the girl was probably just a pawn in a complex game — but who had sent her on the assignment?

THE MARGIN
Ian Stuart

It is rumoured that Walkers Brewery has been selling arms to the South African army, and Graham Lorimer is asked to investigate. He meets the beautiful Shelley van Rynveld, who is dedicated to ending apartheid. When a Walkers employee is killed in a hit-and-run accident, his wife tells Graham that he's been seeing Shelly van Rynveld . . .

TOO LATE FOR THE FUNERAL
Roger Ormerod

Carol Turner, seventeen, and a mystery, is very close to a murder, and she has in her possession a weapon that could prove a number of things. But it is Elsa Mallin who suffers most before the truth of Carol Turner releases her.

NIGHT OF THE FAIR
Jay Baker

The gun was the last of the things for which Harry Judd had fought and now it was in the hands of his worst enemy, aimed at the boy he had tried to help. This was the night in which the past had to be faced again and finally understood.

PAY-OFF IN SWITZERLAND
Bill Knox

'Hot' British currency was being smuggled to Switzerland to be laundered, hidden in a safari-style convoy heading across Europe. Jonathan Gaunt, external auditor for the Queen's and Lord Treasurer's Remembrancer, went along with the safari, posing as a tourist, to get any lead he could. But sudden death trailed the convoy every kilometer to Lake Geneva.

SALVAGE JOB
Bill Knox

A storm has left the oil tanker S. S. *Craig Michael* stranded and almost blocking the only channel to the bay at Cabo Esco. Sent to investigate, marine insurance inspector Laird discovers that the Portuguese bay is hiding a powder keg of international proportions.

BOMB SCARE — FLIGHT 147
Peter Chambers

Smog delayed Flight 147, and so prevented a bomb exploding in mid-air. Walter Keane found that during the crisis he had been robbed of his jewel bag, and Mark Preston was hired to locate it without involving the police. When a murder was committed, Preston knew the stake had grown.

STAMBOUL INTRIGUE
Robert Charles

Greece and Turkey were on the brink of war, and the conflict could spell the beginning of the end for the Western defence pact of N.A.T.O. When the rumour of a plot to speed this possibility reached Counter-espionage in Whitehall, Simon Larren and Adrian Cleyton were despatched to Turkey . . .

CRACK IN THE SIDEWALK
Basil Copper

After brilliant scientist Professor Hopcroft is knocked down and killed by a car, L.A. private investigator Mike Faraday discovers that his death was murder and that differing groups are engaged in a power struggle for The Zetland Method. As Mike tries to discover what The Zetland Method is, corpses and hair-breadth escapes come thick and fast . . .

DEATH OF A MARINE
Charles Leader

When Mike M'Call found the mutilated corpse of a marine in an alleyway in Singapore, a thousand-strong marine battalion was hell-bent on revenge for their murdered comrade — and the next target for the tong gang of paid killers appeared to be M'Call himself . . .